Copyright © Taylor Walker, 2020

Cover Design by SGB Book Cover Designs

First Edition: November 2020
This paperback edition first published in November 2020
This EBook edition first published in November 2020

(Explicit Content)

Chapter 1

This Is How It Goes

As every day does, it starts with the sun rising and waking up in a bed. My parents told me this week that I'm moving to a new school. I start today and I'm feeling nervous. I open my drawers and scan through the many-colored t-shirts. I grab a white t-shirt, then I knock the drawer shut with my hip. I open the drawer below and find my dark blue skinny jeans and a black belt with plain white metal studs; I grab them too and kick the drawer shut. I glance to the right side of the drawers. There sit multiple brands of sneakers and boots on a metal shoe rack. I slowly bend down and grab my high maroon doc martens, I then stumble to the back of my door. There on my door is a wooden coat hanger that holds my coats and some hoodies. I look from left to right and decide on my band hoodie. I pull it down, then drag myself back to my bed and get dressed.

Knock, knock

"Yeah?" I answer as I quickly throw my t-shirt over my head.

"Just checking you're up," Piper says from behind the door.

"Yeah... I'll be down soon," I reply as I bend over to tie my laces.

Piper is my sister she goes to the school that I'm starting today. She is always making sure I'm not late and that I'm always up and ready for breakfast. She makes it a morning routine by lightly knocking when passing my room.

I finish up tying my laces and grab my rucksack from under my bed. I slowly walk to my door and fling it open, I head downstairs. I get to the end of the stairs and throw my bag onto the wooden flooring next to Pipers in the hallway. My dad opens the living room door as I reach for the handle.

"Lync! How many times do I have to tell you about this?" he complains as he grabs his coat from the wall rack.

"More than once?" I say with a smile whilst slowly backing into the living room behind me.

"Come on, get your breakfast. I'm going to work now so I will see you later. Have a good first day!" He smiles as he opens the front door.

"Thanks be safe!" I reply then I dash off into the living room towards the kitchen.

My dad is head of a detective in the police department, so I'm always worrying about him when he goes to work.

I get to the kitchen door and open it slowly. I walk in to see my mum and Piper sat at the table, waiting.

"He's risen!" My mum laughs as she put the bacon into her mouth.

"As always. Right on time." I chuckle as I close the door behind me.

"He wouldn't be awake if it wasn't for me!" Piper points out as she continues chewing on the food in her mouth.

"Urm... I was awake and nearly dressed by the time you knocked." I add walking over to the table.

"Ok kids, eat your breakfast and get going! You don't want to be late for your first day, Lync." My mum stresses.

I nod and grab some toast from the toast rack on the table. My mum always sets the table up neatly every morning.

"You need to stay near me today." Piper sasses as she took a bite from her toast.

"I'm not a baby. I'm old enough to look after myself." I assure her.

"Just listen to Piper please Lync. We want to make sure you settle in fine today." My mum argues.

"Fine." I huff.

I finish my toast and grab a glass from the table. I then reach for the jug of orange juice. I glance over to Piper as I felt her eyes burning into my head.

"What?" I ask.

"You're going to have some fun today." She smirks.

"Don't," I reply.

"Ok, you two that's enough." My mum pipes.

I pour the orange juice into my glass and knock it back in one go. I carefully place the glass back onto the table and quickly make my way to the kitchen door.

"Excuse me, are we forgetting something?" My mum asks.

Piper kisses her on the cheek and then walks towards me.

"Oh, of course!" I chuckle.

I walk back to my mum and lightly kiss her on the cheek. I then head back to the door.

"See you later." Me and Piper say as we open the door.

"Have a good day, you two!" She shouts as we left.

Me and Piper get to the front door and grab our bags. We head out of the front door and walk to school.

"I'm not being funny about you hanging around with me today, you know," Piper explains.

"How can your friends be ok with me tagging along?" I ask.

"They're just laid back like that. They're cool." She answers.

I nod and continue walking. I don't understand why I have to hang around with my older sister. Any other sibling would be against that. But I guess it's only for the first day.

We get to school. Piper spots her friends sat under the old oak tree. We walk over to them.

"Hey!" Her friend shouts.

"Hey!" Piper shouts back.

I have to admit; I felt totally out of place. Surrounded by people I don't know and in an unfamiliar environment.

"Who is this cutie?" Her friend asks with a smile.

"Ew! He's my brother, you creep!" Piper laughs.

"I didn't know you had a brother!" Her friend says.

I don't know where to look. I feel so awkward that one of Piper's friends is making out they have a crush on me.

"Can I go in? I need to sort out my locker and map." I ask.

Piper nods. I slowly drag my feet to the entrance. I feel more anxious than I have ever felt before. I get to the main steps and go up one step at a time. I can feel my heart racing inside my chest. I don't know what to expect here.

I push through the doors and enter the corridor. Everyone is walking up and down or going into their lockers. I feel so out of place here; I don't know anyone. A young teacher approaches me.

"Hello, my name is Miss Jenkins. Are you new here?" She asks sweetly.

"Hi. Yes, it's my first day I'm a little... lost." I smile, followed by a shrug.

"Aww, sure I'll help you. You need to go to the primary office for your map, locker number, and code, and your class number. I can show you if you like?" She says with a smile.

"Yeah sure," I reply bluntly.

Miss Jenkins leads the way down the crowded and loud corridor.

"So what's your name? You look very familiar..." She says whilst looking at me up and down.

"Lync McCarthy, miss," I reply.

"You look a lot like an old friend of mine. He had dark hair and blue eyes. Whereas you have blonde hair and green eyes." She adds.

"Many people have said that to me actually... what was his name?" I ask.

"I would tell you, but no one who remembers him is allowed to say his name. Especially here on the school grounds." She answers politely.

"Oh ok, that's fine," I mutter.

We approach a door with a golden plaque which read:

School Office

"There you go, Lync. I may see you in class." She chuckles.

I nod and knock on the wooden door.

"Come in." A voice shouts from behind the door.

I slowly push the handle down and nuzzle the door open.

"Lync McCarthy, sir. I'm a new student." I announce to him.

"Ah, yes. Come over to my desk, sir. We will arrange everything for you." He instructs.

I walk over to his desk and watch him digging through his drawers for the paperwork.

"Here's your file! Let me have a glance..." He insists.

I watch his facial expressions change almost immediately. His jaw drops as he scans through my information. The way he's reacting makes me feel I have done something wrong.

"How is this possible?" He whispers to himself.

"Sorry sir, I didn't catch that?" I question.

"Nothing young sir. I've just read something that I thought wasn't true. Nothing bad." He explains politely.

"Anyway, here is your map, timetable for lessons, locker number, and code. I hope you have a fantastic first day!" He says cheerfully. I step back slowly.

"Thanks, sir. I'll try..." I reply as I carefully reverse to the door.

I stand in front of my locker and stare at it. I feel a slight chill running down my spine. Something doesn't feel right about this locker. I know it's a locker, but I have a feeling of uncertainty. As I'm about to put my new code in, a random student appears next to me to get into their locker.

"I wouldn't trust that locker." The student says as he flings open his locker door and scampers through his books, which are sat neatly inside.

"What's so bad about it?" I ask.

"The devil's locker. That's all I'm saying." He replies hesitantly.

"Oh..." I say with a confused look on my face.

"If you want to know more, meet me at the old oak tree at lunch." He grumbles as he threw his books into his rucksack.

Before I could answer him he slams the locker door shut and speeds down the corridor whilst trying to shuffle his bag onto his shoulder.

"That's weird..." I whisper to myself.

I walk through the door of my first lesson. English. I somehow found the class using the map instead of asking everyone around me. I stroll over to a desk and notice everyone looking at me strangely like I was an alien, not a new student. I pull the chair out, throw my bag under the desk, and sit down. My ears start to burn; I can hear people whispering around me. I turn to look to my right and a girl stood there looking at me.

"Excuse me?" The girl asks politely.

"Yeah?" I quickly reply.

"Do you have a brother called Killian?" She asks.

A strange feeling happens, I instantly feel sick and become lightheaded. I can't explain it it's just a weird feeling I have.

"No. I have a sister." I splutter.

The girl nods and walks back to her desk. Why did I feel the way I did when she asks that? Killian... Who is he?

"Psst!" A guy behind me sounded to get my attention. I look over.

"The reason she asks that is that you look like Killian Saunders." He whispers.

"Who is he?" I ask quietly.

"I will tell you later." He whispers back.

I turn to the front of the class to look at the whiteboard. There stood Miss Jenkins she looks directly at me. I could see the fear in her facial expression. I look away and look out the classroom window. I feel unwelcome, I feel like I have done something wrong.

Class finishes and Miss Jenkins begins to pile together with the classwork, books, and files. I follow the class to the door. I got closer and closer to her desk, I feel a sudden rush of anxiety.

"Lync, can you wait behind one moment, please?" She asks kindly.

"Err... Sure." I shrug as I got to the front of her desk.

I stand and watch the other students walking through the door into the corridor. I can't help but feel scared.

It didn't take long for the last student to leave the room, Miss Jenkins walks to the door and closes it quietly. I watch her as she makes her way back to the desk and sits down on her chair. She crosses her legs and shuffles her chair to the desk.

"So Lync, I see I have you for class." She says sweetly.

"I guess so..." I reply.

"You probably won't remember me." She adds.

"Nope. You're right, I don't recognize you." I add.

"You are one lucky young man. It is truly a miracle you're still here." She chirps.

I now feel that something is not adding up. First, people were asking weird questions, now Miss Jenkins tells me she knows me.

"Do you know where your scars came from on your neck and stomach?" She asks.

"A car accident when I was 12," I explain.

"Ah. Well, you're very lucky. You can go to your next lesson now." She continues.

I look at Miss Jenkins, confused. What is she trying to tell me? I turn around and walk to the classroom door, I grab the handle and drag it down.

"So who is Killian Saunders?" I ask before opening the door.

There's a long pause, then Miss Jenkins responds to my question.

"Just an Urban Legend, Mr. McCarthy." She reassures.

Soon enough it was lunch break. I walk to the front of the school to meet the strange guy from the lockers this morning. I want to find out why everyone is being so strange to me. I stop at the steps and look around for the old oak tree. I look to my left and it's there, so is the weird dude and his friends.

"Over here, new kid!" He shouts.

I plod over him. I feel nervous about this. What is he going to say? What is he going to tell me?

"Hey. So what's the story behind my locker?" I ask.

"Before we go into the story, I have my friends that want to know more about the Urban Legend." He interrupts.

"My name is Trey. This is Callie and Deccan." He continues.

"Nice to meet you all." I smile.

"You too." Callie smiles back.

"Your locker..." He starts. "It's the locker of the actual devil himself, Killian Saunders." He explains.

"Who is this dude? Why is everyone asking me if he's my brother?" I snap.

"We cannot mention him who shall not be named on school grounds Trey!" Callie shrieks.

"Callie, he needs to know like everyone else here." He replies calmly.

"Apparently according to his detailed description he looked a lot like you but with black hair and blue eyes. You even have his dress sense." He adds.

"What is so bad about him he can't be mentioned?" I ask.

"According to the Urban Legend, he murdered over 20 students at this school. He killed the first 3 as revenge. After he did that he murdered his family including his little brother." He explains.

"Wow... so he was a psychopath?" I mutter.

"Yes, yes, he was." He grumbles.

"What was his brother's name?" I continue to question.

"His name was Lockie Saunders. He was sweet. He was the quiet type. The opposite of Killian." Callie interrupts.

Suddenly, I feel as if I'm going to faint.

"Are you ok? You look, pale dude." Deccan asks.

"Yeah, I just need to sit down." I slur as I try to sit down but then I collapse.

Chapter 2

This Will Be The Death of Me

I awoke in the school's nurses' office. I look around and no one is there. I look to my right side and see handcuffs attached around my right wrist. I pull and pull, but it's locked onto the bed rail. The nurse and doctor enter the room.

"Hello Lync, how are you feeling?" The nurse asks.

"I'm ok. I just want to know if you cuff other students to the bed rail after they faint?" I ask.

"You're a funny kid, Mr. McCarthy. I take it you find yourself as the class clown." The doctor interrupts.

"I'm more on the quiet side unless you do something to me that is unnecessary like this." I point out as I tug on the handcuff around my wrist.

"I can fix that problem if you can speak to me without your attitude." He grumbles.

"Well, realistically speaking doctor, you shouldn't have cuffed me to the bed. It was unnecessary for the situation I have just been in." I explain.

Suddenly my dad walks through the door of the nurses' office. He closes the door behind him. He then looks at me in shock.

"Well, Lync, we need to take precautions." He continues.

"What precautions? I'm 17 years old for god sake! All I did was faint!" I scream.

"Uncuff my son, please sir." My dad asks politely.

"I can't risk that detective. I'm not one for taking any risks anymore." He snorts.

"Well let's talk about this away from my son please sir. I have just asked you politely to uncuff my son." My dad demands.

The doctor huffs and walks over to me. He reaches into his left pocket for the keys and unlocks the cuffs from around my wrist.

"As I said, doctor, it was unnecessary," I say as I climb off the bed.

"He needs checking over at the hospital detective. He could have the curse." The doctor shouts.

"I know my son better than anyone else. He doesn't need your help. He is a normal, happy, 17-year-old, leave him be." My dad explains.

"Lync, go to class I need to speak to the doctor alone." My dad demands.

I nod and proceed to the door. As I reach for the door I turn to look at the doctor, my dad, and the nurse. I wonder what they want to talk about without me being around? I open the door and exit the room. Why are they being so secretive?

My traumatic first school day comes to an end. I wait at the old oak tree for Trey, Callie, and Deccan so I could let them know that I'm ok. As I turn to look at the entrance, I see them exit the building. I wave my arm in the air to get their attention.

"Lync, you're ok!" Callie screams in excitement.

"I guess I am." I chuckle.

"Glad you're a good dude. We are heading out for urban hunt tonight if you would like to join?" Trey asks.

"Why do you want to look into something that could be real and dangerous? If it's a dead story leave it that way. Reason it being an urban legend dude." I explain.

"No one knows if it's real or not Lync. This is why we want to investigate it properly." Deccan adds.

"I understand that man, but you could be risking your lives. What if it isn't some stupid urban legend? What if this Killian dude is real and murders you?" I caution.

"Lync... it's not real!" Trey interrupts.

"How do you know if it's real Lync? The story of him killing his family, friends, and other school students and stuff doesn't add up. How can he get away with it and not get caught by the police?" Deccan snaps.

"Dude, I'm not standing here arguing about a stupid urban legend," I mutter as I began to walk away.

"Lync don't go! They're just being jerks." Callie shouts.

"Friendly advice Callie, do not go on the urban hunt with them," I warn.

I gave Callie my number if she needs me for any reason regarding any hunts. I didn't want her to involve herself but if she is forced to go, I'm going too.

"Give me a text or call and I will get to you ok?" I whisper.

Callie smiles and nods. I continue to make my way home.

I got to my front door and quickly open it. As soon as I step inside I throw my bag onto the floor in the hall. I slowly but quietly close the door.

"Lync is that you darling?" My mum shouts from the living room.

"Yeah, mum. It's just me." I respond.

I open the living room door and see that my mum was sat in her special brown leather chair. My dad was lay on the black leather settee.

"Did you have a good first day?" My mum asks. My dad hadn't told her about the nurses' office.

"Yeah, not great but not bad," I answer.

My mum smiles and continues watching TV. I turn to look at my dad. I try to give him a look to hint 'what happened about communication?' he just shrugs. I didn't want to be around for when he does tell my mum so I think it would be best if I go out for a while.

"I'm going to go out on my skates for a bit," I tell my mum as I open the living room door.

"No problem sweetheart. Be careful!" She says cheerfully.

I walk out of the living room and close the door. I head upstairs to my bedroom to get my inclines. I open the bedroom door and go straight over to my wardrobe. I grab my skates from the bottom and close the doors, I quickly run downstairs. I open the front door and sit down to put my skates on.

"You need to speak to me about what happened Lync." My dad mumbles. I jump in fright.

"You need to stop sneaking up behind me!" I yell.

"What happened before you fainted? Be honest." My dad asks sternly.

"I just went lightheaded and tried to sit down. That's all I remember." I explain.

"Nothing strange happened? Hallucinations or anything?" He pushes.

"No? Can you just stop going into detail about things!" I shout as I pull my skates tight.

"You have a meeting with someone tomorrow before school. I'll be taking you to the appointment." My dad adds.

"Ok," I reply.

I stood up and grab my earphones from my pocket.

"Anyone told you anything at school that you didn't know about?" My dad challenges

I plug my earphones into my ears and then plug them into my phone. I scroll to my skating playlist and press play.

"Sorry, what was that? I can't hear you!" I say loudly.

My dad gives me a stern look and shakes his head. I skate down the path onto the road.

I get to the skate park which isn't far from home. I start to do tricks and jumps on the skate ramps. Suddenly my phone rings. It's a number that isn't saved on my phone. I press answer.

"Hello?" I answer.

"Lync it's Callie I need to meet you somewhere urgently!" She cries.

"Callie, what's going on? Are you ok?" I ask, trying to stay calm.

"I should have listened to you! Where are you?" She asks.

"I'm at the skate park. Can you meet me here or do you want me to meet you?" I ask her.

"No! Stay there! It's really bad I can't let you get involved." She shouts.

"Ok. Keep texting me until you get here." I suggest.

"I will." Callie replies.

She hangs up. I skate as fast as I can to the entrance of the park.

(Callie: I'm 5 minutes away!)

(Me: Hurry up I'm waiting at the entrance.)

(Callie: I'm trying!)

(Me: Try harder. I'm worried about you!)

Callie didn't reply. My heart stopped. Why is she not replying?

I quickly skate out onto the path and look both ways. There's no sign of her. I take a lucky guess and skate towards Dead Man's Woods direction. In the distance I see Callie.

"Callie!" I shout as I wave my arms in the air to get her attention.

"Lync! Stay there!" She cries.

"No! I'm coming to you!" I shout. I race over to her as fast as I can.

I reach Callie and see her sitting on the path with her back against a wall. Something bad must have happened.

"What the hells happened?" I yell.

"We did the psycho dare!" She cries.

"I told you not to go on that stupid hunt!" I continue to yell.

"I know! I'm so sorry Lync, but we're cursed now he will be coming for us!" She cries.

"Come on, stand up," I say calmly. I help her up.

"Behind you! He's there! He's real!" Callie screams in horror.

I turn to look behind me. No one was there. I turn to look at Callie again. She has her hands on her face, crying in fear.

"Callie? No one is there." I reassure.

"He's coming. He's going to kill me! Please help me!" She screams.

I grab her and hug her. I wrap my arms tightly around her. The road is silent, I feel a cold breeze pass my left cheek. No one was there in the flesh but maybe someone was watching from the other side.

"I believe you," I whisper into Callie's ear.

"Is he still here?" I whisper again.

She slowly lifts her head from my chest and looks behind me and then turns to look behind her.

"No, he's gone." She says calmly.

"What about Trey and Deccan?" I ask.

"They did it too but Trey's dad is into all that voodoo hypnotist stuff." She explains.

"Any curse or bad spirits his dad can fix it, but they left me." She sighs.

"Seriously? You need better friends." I say.

"Like you?" She smiles.

"If you consider me as a friend yeah." I laugh.

"Come on let's get you home." I insist. Callie smiles and leads the way.

So this must be why my dad asks about hallucinations. The psycho curse causes it.

We get to the front of Callie's house. She looks up at her house then she looks back at me.

"Could you not sneakily stay over tonight?" She asks.

"I think we would get caught out." I laugh.

"I would feel safer if you were with me. Please Lync!" She begs.

I look at her house and then look back at her. I can see the twinkle in her eyes. It's the type that kind of makes you want to do what she asks. But it's too risky.

"If I stayed here your dad would kill me. If I didn't turn up home my dad and the police will be out looking for me." I explain.

"I understand." She replies bluntly.

"I can video call you. We can stay on video call all night it's the same... is." I laugh.

"It's a deal!" Callie says happily.

I smile. She opens her front gate and quietly shuts it behind her. She slowly walks up her path to her front door. She turns to me and waves. I wave back. She smiles and opens the front door then closes it. I take off on my skates to get back home.

I get to my front door and untie my skates. Suddenly my dad opens the door.

"Where have you been?" He shouts.

"I met a friend that was upset, is that ok?" I ask.

"Next time tell us what time you will be home. You had us worried!" He snaps. He then shuts the door on me.

"World's greatest father award goes to your dad," I mumble to myself.

I finally get my skates off and open the front door. I shut it with my foot then run up the stairs. I push my bedroom door open with my foot and threw my skates down next to my door. I walk over to my bed, sit down then grab my laptop from underneath. I log in and go onto a video call with Callie. She answers.

"I didn't think you would do this." She says as she yawns.

"Why not?" I ask.

"Just the way Trey and Deccan are." She replies.

"I'm not them." I murmur.

"Of course." She giggles.

"Just give me a minute I need to get undressed for bed," I say. Callie nods.

I move away from the laptop out of the camera shot to take my clothes off. I throw my t-shirt over my head and unbutton my jeans. As I'm just pulling them off I hear static on the call. I quickly throw them across the room and grab my lounge pants and hop over to the laptop as I pull them up.

"Callie are you there?" I panic.

The static starts to disappear.

"Shhh." She whispers.

I look closely at her camera to see a shadow in the corner of her bedroom.

"Callie, get the hell out of there!" I shout.

"I can't. It's near my door." She whispers as tears stream down her cheeks.

"House phone number now! Type it or something!" I yell.

She begins to type as I watch the shadow. The house number comes through. I grab my laptop and carry it with me to grab my phone from my jeans pocket. The shadow doesn't move. I begin typing the number in my phone as well as glancing at Callie in the call. I feel horrible that I can't do more to help her. I press call on my phone and it begins to ring. Callie's mum answers.

"Hello?" She says.

"Hi this is Callie's friend can you please check on her in her room? She's upset." I say hoping that it would work.

"Err... Sure I'll go up now." She says. Then she hangs up.

"You're ok Callie I promise!" I reassure her.

The shadow then starts walking towards Callie.

"Callie behind you!" I yell.

Callie screams and the call ends. I close my laptop and throw it onto my bed. I grab my t-shirt and put it back on. I run downstairs and begin to get my vans on. My mum opens the living room door.

"Lync, it's past your curfew." My mum reminds me.

"I don't care it's urgent!" I snap.

"Well, I do." She adds as she locks the front door and removes the key.

"Are you being serious?" I shout.

"Get to your room." She says sternly.

Usually, I obey my parents but this isn't the time to obey.

"No," I mumble.

"What did you just say?" She growls.

"I say no!" I snap.

"Kevin, sort Lync out now!" She screams to my dad in the kitchen.

I run past her through the living room into the kitchen. I grab the handle of the back door and open it.

"You dare leave this house!" My dad bellows.

I turn around and smile at him and run out the door into the backyard.

"Lync get back here this instance!" My dad yells as he approaches the back door.

I continue to ignore him and throw open the back gate.

I finally get to Callie's and the lights are on in the house. I rush to the door and knock. Callie's brother answers the door.

"Errr... Hi. I wanted to see if Callie is ok? I was on a video call and it cut out. I'm really worried about her." I explain.

"Are you her new boyfriend?" He asks.

"No... I'm a friend." I answer.

"Anyway, is she ok?" I ask.

"My mums with her. We are waiting for an ambulance." He grumbles.

"Please let me see her!" I yell.

He opens the door and moves out of the way. I run upstairs.

"First bedroom!" He shouts.

I open the door to find Callie's mum in tears and Callie bleeding.

"I knew it! Why didn't I listen to her?" I cry.

"Was this your doing?" Her mum sniffs.

"No, she went to Dead Man's Woods with Trey and Deccan. I told her not to go and do anything stupid!" I cry.

"What did she do?" Her mum asks.

"The psycho dare which then gives you the psycho curse," I explain.

"Don't tell me it's to do with that stupid urban legend?" She begs.

"Yes... it is." I reply.

Callie's mum continues to cry as she cradles her daughter's unconscious, bloody body. I have never felt so guilty in my entire life. Suddenly I hear police sirens and ambulance. I quickly run out of the bedroom and downstairs. Of course, my dad is going to be here.

"Lync, what the hell are you doing here?" He yells as he slams the car door shut and walks towards me.

"I told you it was urgent! I'm sorry I wanted to help a friend." I cry as I run over.

My dad then whistles to his colleague.

"Take Lync to the station. I want a full witness statement and interview from him." He demands.

His colleague nods and walks to the car. I look at my dad, all I can see is disappointment. I put my head down in shame and follow his colleague to the car.

11:25pm. I'm sitting in the police station in the interview room waiting for my dad's colleague to interview me. I can't believe I've got myself in this predicament. Then he walks through the door.

"How can you be so stupid Lync?" He asks as he walks over to the chair.

"I wanted to see if she was ok. She's my friend." I answer.

"Well let's find out what happened. Start from the very start." He begins.

"I finished school, got home then went out on my skates," I say.

"Then what happened next?" He asks.

"I went to the skate park 10 minutes away from home. I went on for about 20 minutes until I got a hysteric phone call from Callie." I reply.

"Why was she hysterical? What did she say?" He questions as he writes everything down.

"She was crying and panicking. She sounded scared like something bad had happened. She says she needed to meet me somewhere urgently." I explain.

"What action did you take?" He asks.

"I told her I was at the skate park and if she could meet me there or if she wanted me to meet up with her wherever she was. She then shouts at me to stay at the skate park as she didn't want me to get involved." I continue.

"Involved in what?" He queries as he continues to write down everything I was saying.

"Well I began to text her until she got to me but she stopped texting so I panicked. I skated down to the road to look for her and she wasn't there. I then skated in the direction of Dead Man's Woods and I saw her less than a few minutes away sat on the path crying." I answer.

"What did she tell you when you got there?" He asks.

"She told me that her Trey and Deccan went on the urban hunt. I told her she was stupid for doing it. She told me that her, Trey, and Deccan have the psycho curse and that he would be coming for them. But Trey and Deccan went to Trey's dad to remove their curse. They left her." I explain.

"Psycho curse?" He asks.

Little did I know my dad is watching the whole thing behind the mirror screen.

"Yeah to do with the urban legend..." I reply. "She told me she could see him and began to scream and cry so I hug her. I couldn't see anything myself but she was terrified. Afterward, I walked her home and she begged me to stay over but I knew my dad and her family wouldn't allow it. I told her I would video-call her as soon as I got home, which I did." I trail off.

"And this curse unravelled on the video call?" He queries as he takes notes again.

"I walked out of the camera shot as I went to get changed for bed. I heard static coming from the call so I ran over to see what was happening. When I looked on her side there was a shadow in the corner of her room. She froze in fear. All I could see were tears streaming down her face." I explain.

"Then I got her to give me her home number, I rang and told her mum to check on her. No longer as she hung up the call cut out. So I got partially dressed and ran out of the house to hers. That's when I discovered what had happened." I continue.

"So you didn't take part in the urban hunt?" He asks.

"No, because you don't know if it's real or not. urban legends should never be investigated... it's too risky." I add.

My dad's colleague nods and ends the interview. He then stands up and pulls together the paperwork. He walks to the door and leaves the room. I sit quietly in the interview room. My dad walks in through the door.

"Dad! I'm so sorry I know I always listen to you and I know I've messed up big time." I cry as I stand up.

"It's ok Lync. You were just looking out for a friend which is understandable. I heard everything." He says with a smile. "Good news is your friend will be ok. Minor wounds. She was lucky." He announces.

"Did you find who it was?" I ask.

"We have an idea yes. But if they do anything like this I don't want you getting involved ok?" He states.

"Yeah, I won't." I answer.

Chapter 3

Who Is Lockie Saunders?

Me and my dad get home at specifically 1.30 am. The incident happened at 8 pm. It was a long night for both of us. For him being at the scene and watching my interview. For me being in the middle of this mess, then being interviewed and staying at the station until my dad finished. It was chaos.

"I'll see you in the morning, son. Nice work tonight, that girl may not have made it through the night if you didn't do what you did." He praises.

"Thanks, dad. I still feel like I could have done more to save her from being in that situation." I sniff.

"You can't always help everyone Lync, if you want to be in the force, you need to know that. You did me proud tonight with your actions. You're proving yourself." He admits.

"Thanks, Dad," I mumble as I walk upstairs.

I get to my bedroom, the door is still open. I walk in and look around and see the clothes I left on the floor and my laptop on my bed, how I left it. I rush to my bed and flip my laptop open. I click on the search engine. I search 'Killian

Saunders urban legend'. It come up immediately with news headlines and photos of the house, school, and Killian.

"What the hell?" I mutter to myself.

I go on to the first link. 'Saunders Murder' I scroll down. Saunders bodies were found at the scene.

Lillian Saunders age 47, Charles Saunders age 50, and Lockie Saunders age 12. Bodies were discovered by a neighbor who says the scene was gruesome and looked as if it was done out of anger. Killian Saunders' body was not discovered at the scene. Which places him as the prime suspect.

I stop reading and scroll down to see if there is any photos of the family. I find one of Killian. Everyone in school were right... I look like him, just different eye color and hair color. I close the tab and open a new one to search for images. 'Lockie Saunders' the page loads up. The first photo is Lockie's school photo. It click on it. Suddenly I drop my laptop on the floor and it lands with a bang. I run over to my desk and yank my drawer open. I dig to the back of the drawer for my photo album from when I was 13. I grab it, run back to my laptop, and open it. I compare the photos...

"Holy shit..." I whisper.

"Lockie isn't dead, I'm Lockie!" I yell.

I quickly flick through the photos to check. The eye color, hair color, freckles, all match. Suddenly I begin getting flashbacks of that night.

"Goodnight, little brother."

"I'm not tired…"

"Killian, please! I love you! You're my big brother! Please don't hurt me!"

"Help! Mum! Dad!"

"Goodnight, sleep tight."

I come out of the flashback, clenching my chest. I struggle to breathe. My chest is tight, tears streaming down my face. Then I run over to my wardrobe mirror and throw my t-shirt off over my head. I run my fingers over my neck scar then the scars on my stomach.

"I'm adopted… my parents are dead… my brother is a psychopath…" I whisper to myself.

"It's not a stupid urban legend, it's real. I'm part of it." I cry.

Suddenly my dad flings the bedroom door open. Standing behind him is my mum and Piper. They all look at me then their eyes slowly drift to my laptop and photo album.

"So when the hell were you going to tell me?" I scream.

"Just calm down son, I don't know what you think you've seen but you're not Lockie." My dad says calmly as he approaches me.

"Don't lie to me! I remember that night Killian tried to murder me!" I yell.

"Lync, breathe sweetheart." My mum whispers.

"Breathe? I'm supposed to be dead to the world! How could I not remember this?" I continue to yell.

"Mum? Dad? He isn't stupid, you've been caught out." Piper butts in.

"Thank you, Piper!" I shout.

"I'll keep my name as Lync as I'm guessing it's witness protection?" I add.

"Yes, it is." My dad answers.

"By rights now you are my family. You are my parents and Piper is my sister. But you can't hide the truth forever." I explain.

"He is right Kevin; he needs to learn who he is." My mum admits.

"I want you to call me Lockie at home. It will help me remember, but in public, I will use Lync." I announce.

"It may be a little hard but sure son." My dad sighs.

"If you want to try and bring Killian in you need me. Me as in Lockie." I demand.

"Sure but we need to make sure you're safe more than anything." He replies.

"I know." I smile.

"Ok sweetheart, we will leave you to go to bed. Leave the laptop tonight please." My mum stresses.

"No worries. Goodnight." I say with a smile.

Everyone leaves and my dad closes my door. Now it all makes sense. I have to go on these urban hunts.

Morning arrives. I wake up and stretch over to grab my phone. It's 7 am. I throw my phone and flop back onto my bed.

"Lockie! Get up!" Piper shouts.

"I'm not in school this morning, I have an appointment," I yell back.

There's no reply. I pull myself up to a sitting position. I look down at my scars again.

"How did I survive this?" I ask myself.

I sigh then climb out of bed. I walk over to my wardrobe and grab my blue skinny jeans and a white t-shirt. I then grab my high maroon doc martens. I stumble to my drawers for socks and underwear then make my way over to my bed and begin to get dressed. I finish up by tying my laces and slowly walk to my bedroom door. I grab the handle and open it. The landing was clear. I head downstairs into the living room then into the kitchen.

"Morning darling. How are you feeling?" My mum asks.

"Weird... I feel like everything is catching up to me." I explain.

"We will mention it to Quin when we meet him soon." My dad interrupts.

"Who's Quin?" I ask.

"He took all your memories as they were too traumatic for you to deal with when you were 12." Piper states.

"You didn't have to say it like that Piper." My dad snaps.

"It's fine dad, I prefer it that way and not sugar-coated." I laugh.

I grab some cereal from the side and then grab a bowl. I begin to pour the cereal.

"I never imagined I would ask you this. But would you like to come to work with me today and have a look at the files?" My dad asks politely.

"Sure, I know it's going to be upsetting remembering everything but I need to," I explain.

I pour the milk into my bowl of cereal. I pull open the cutlery drawer for a spoon.

"So are you going to use Lockie as bait for Killian?" Piper chirps.

"Piper!" My mum and dad shout.

"What? It's an idea." She adds as she shrugs.

"She isn't wrong... Killian would recognize me from a mile off." I say as I scoop a spoonful of cereal into my mouth.

"Don't be absurd. That's the stupidest thing you two have ever said." My mum scolds as she takes a sip of her coffee.

I and Piper look at each other and smirk. It's a great idea in our eyes.

"Come on then Lockie, let's go and see Quin." My dad says as he stands from the table.

I finish my cereal and go out the kitchen door into the living room. I get to the front door and open it. I wait for my dad on the drive.

"You look nervous." My dad points out.

"I am," I answer.

We get into the car. I pull my seatbelt across my chest. I wonder what Quin will be like?

We arrive at Quin's house. I begin to get nervous. I may get my memories back which will help my dad. But I know it won't be pleasant memories. I remember from my flashback, I couldn't see Killian's face.

"Are you ready then?" My dad asks as he opens the car door.

"Sure..." I sigh as remove my seatbelt and open my door.

We get out of the car and walk over to the house. The more I overthink the more nervous I become. My dad presses the doorbell and my heart begins to race. Suddenly the door opens, Trey answers.

"You evil..." I start. My dad grabs my t-shirt.

"Leave it!" He says sternly.

"Erm... dad it's for you!" Trey yells.

I hear someone running down the stairs. A young-looking guy came to the door. He looks like he's in his 30's but that wouldn't be possible with the age Trey is.

"Lync, nice to see you again. Let's go into my office." He chirps.

We step into his house and follow him to his office. I can't help but keep looking at my dad as we follow Quin.

"It's ok son, I'm here and I'm staying here." He reassures me.

We walk into Quin's office. He closes the door behind us. My dad leads me to the black leather chair and I sit down. He walks over to sit with Quin on the blue plastic chairs.

"So Lync how are you feeling?" Quin asks politely.

"Scared," I admit.

"Why?" He asks.

"I remember." I splutter.

"How did that happen, Kevin?" He turns to my dad.

"Tried researching something and put two and two together and realized who he was." My dad replies.

"It's not his fault, I want to remember. I'm ready to." I shout.

"Lync. If I was to allow the memories back it would be too much. Trust me." Quin argues.

"I just want to be me. I need to know about my past. Please. I'm ready." I beg.

"Trust him, Quin. I'm here and I have EMT on speed dial." My dad adds.

"Ok, if you're sure." He sighs.

"Yes," I answer.

I take a deep breath to try and relax. My heart is still pounding as if it's going to break through my chest. I shake uncontrollably as I know that these memories aren't going to be nice.

"I'm just warning you both. I don't feel from Lync's energy that he is mentally prepared for this." Quin warns us.

"Just do what you've got to do. He's my responsibility and it's what he wants." My dad snaps.

"Ok, Lync? I want you to close your eyes." He says softly. I then close my eyes.

"Now I need you to relax, let all them tense feelings float away. Inhale through your nose and slowly exhale from your mouth." He continues.

"Good. Now repeat that for me." He says softly.

"How do you feel?" He asks.

"I feel relaxed," I reply.

"Good. Now I want you to say your real name in your head. Repeat this 5 times." He whispers.

"Have you done that?" He asks quietly.

"Yes..." I answer.

"Now. Lockie. Open your eyes and look at me." He asks.

I slowly open my eyes and I begin to feel weird. Quin slowly stands up and stands in front of me.

"Good. Now close your eyes and start from the beginning. The journey to Florida, your new home, the first day. Let all that flow right back to you." He whispers.

Suddenly I begin to get flashbacks, they start rushing back to me. The day I was excited to get to our new house.

My mum... she looked beautiful. My dad happily singing. Killian... Staring out of his window. The 3-day argument when I cried to Killian. Then the memories of the hospital. And the bad memories begin to rush in. I start to scream but I couldn't open my eyes.

"Make it stop! I can't do this!" I scream as the tears stream down my cheeks.

"It can't be stopped, Lockie." Quin replies.

"It's ok son you can do this." My dad encourages. Then the final memory, Killian trying to murder me. His face… is horrifying.

"Pull me out of it now!" I scream.

My dad looks at Quin.

"That's not the final part Lockie. You see Killian again." He replies.

Suddenly the flashbacks pause and everything goes black. Then I remember walking home from school. Killian knew I still went to that stupid middle school. He chased me home laughing and screaming. He said he was going to finish the job. I begin screaming more and more to the point my throat began to sting and my voice cracks. I feel the tears trickling down my cheeks.

"Pull him out of it now Quin! This is torcher!" My dad yells.

"If I pull him out now it could make him worse. I warned you, he isn't prepared." He grumbles.

I continue screaming over them talking it was too much to take in. Then it stops. I take a deep breath and fall off the chair.

"Lync!" My dad shouts as he runs over to me. I open my eyes, I don't feel the same anymore.

"What happened?" I ask.

"Relax Lockie. You're safe." Quin reassures me.

"Why did you call me Lync?" I ask my dad.

"It's the name you need to use at school remember so Killian can't find you." He explains.

"Oh yeah," I answer.

"I have a headache," I say as I place my hand onto my head.

"That's completely normal. You're unique Lockie. You've just managed to cope with all the memories, I didn't think you could do it." Quin says with a smile as he folds his arms.

"I'm more capable than people think," I say as I stand up.

"Just people don't believe me... dad," I smirk. My dad smiles and helps me up. It was nice to be back to my normal self but the images of my mum and dad will never go away. And Killian's face... unforgettable.

Chapter 4

Doctor Creep

I sit in the car as my dad is in the station to check if it's ok for me to be with him in his office. I can't wait to look through the files. As I wait, I call Callie to see how she is.

"Lync! I'm so glad you rang me!" She says excitedly.

"Well, you sound better!" I laugh.

"I may sound better, but I'm still in pain." She sighs.

"You'll be up and about in no time. Just make sure you relax and recover first." I advise.

"How long do you think it will be until I'm up and walking?" She asks.

"2 weeks but healing time is around a month or just over," I explain.

"Wow... how do you know that?" She gasps.

"I know someone who went through it." I laugh.

"Could you visit me?" She asks politely.

"Sure, I'll come over to the hospital later," I reply.

"Good! Make sure you do." She giggles.

"I will, I promise. I never break promises. But I'm going to have to go cause my dad is on his way back." I say.

"No problem, Lync. I'll see you later!" She says followed by an excited squeal.

"See you later." I chuckle. I hang up and my dad opens my door.

"Who was on the phone?" He asks.

"Callie. She wants me to visit her later." I propose.

"Ah, that's nice of you. Anyway, you can come to my office and see what we have so far." My dad explains. I nod and climb out of the car. I take a few steps forward to the headquarters. I look at the building it's humongous.

"Come on then, son, let's go." My dad insists. As we walk away my dad locks the car behind us.

It doesn't take us long to get to the main doors. We stroll inside and walk into the lift.

"So why have you not caught him yet?" I ask.

"Because he disappears and then we cannot locate him." My dad answers.

"You know he is human, not a ghost." I smile.

"Not as easy as you think, Lync." My dad sighs.

The lift doors open and my dad steps out, I follow behind. I look around me and police officers begin nodding at me and smiling. I give a slight smile back, I turn to look at where my dad is, he stood waiting at his office door. I hasten to him. He unlocks the door, then we walk in. I quietly close the door behind me.

"Another question." I imply.

"Go on..." My dad says with a smile.

"Why did you adopt me?" I ask. My dad paused and turns to look at me.

"You had no one, and you went through a lot. I felt I had a purpose to protect you." He answers.

"Don't be a cheesy dad." I laugh as I walk over to sit on the chair in front of his desk.

"It's true!" He continues.

"Behave." I chuckle. I grab a file from the case box and open it up. Ironically it was my file.

"Wow..." I gasp.

"Your wounds? They were pretty bad weren't they?" My dad pipes. I have a flashback again.

"Are we ok to take some photos, Lockie?"

"Yeah..."

"They're pretty bad aren't they?"

"They were worse before the doctors stitched them."

"Of course they were."

"When can I come home with you?"

"Soon."

I come back around panting, trying to breathe again.

"You remember that night we took the photos didn't you?" My dad ask, I nod.

"Here have a glass of water." My dad says as he hands me the glass. I begin taking sips.

"You don't need to read your file. It's mainly for evidence against Killian and your witness protection record." My dad adds.

I push the file towards him. I've had enough torcher for today with memories and flashbacks. I want to know how Killian turned out.

"Can you give me Killian's file please?" I cough.

"Of course. Here." My dad replies as he passes me Killian's file.

I open it up and find all his personal information. I read into his medical report.

"Do you know if I have the same illness?" I question.

"Don't worry son. You are too good and kind you don't have any of the traits Killian had." He explains.

"That's good to know." I trail off.

I read into how many times he needed to be sedated. How much medication he was taking. The number of rage frenzy's he had, the list went on.

"It's ringing alarm bells just reading this. Why did they continue to treat him like a normal teenager?" I yell.

"Because they believed he could be fixed until they realized he couldn't. That's when everything began to go downhill with him." My dad explains.

"Well, I don't need to read anymore." I sigh as I push the file back to him.

"How many murders has he committed since my family?" I ask.

"Eight. All to do with the psycho dare as people have says when being interviewed." He grumbles.

"Oh..." I say followed by a gulp.

"Anyway, I need to go see Callie. Would you mind dropping me off at the hospital?" I ask politely.

"Sure." He answers as he stands from his desk.

I open the door and wait for my dad just outside of his office. I watch all the officers and detectives working. Then my dad walks out of his office and locks it. He leads the way back to the lift.

"So, is Callie your new girlfriend?" My dad asks followed by a chuckle.

"No... she's a friend dad." I reply awkwardly.

The lift arrives and the doors open. We both step in and my dad leans over to the buttons and presses the ground floor.

"You care for her an awful lot." He chirps.

"That's what friends do dad," I say bluntly.

"Don't get sour with me now Lockie!" He laughs.

I shake my head and wait until we get to the ground floor. We exit the lift and head towards the main doors.

"For father and son's sake, if you do get a girlfriend you're ok to speak to me about it. I'd rather that than you get up to no good... if you know what I mean." He explains.

"Yes, dad I know what you mean." I huff.

We get to the car. I stand at the door and wait until my dad unlocks it. I turn to look at the trees... Killian is standing there. Watching. He has his hood up and his hands in his pockets, he lifts his head slightly to reveal his huge carved smile.

"Err... dad? Killian is by the trees." I whisper.

He looks at me then glances over to the trees.

"So he is. Don't worry he isn't here for you." He reassures.

"Who is he watching then?" I ask.

"Me. I've been trying to track him down since your family's murder. He knows I'm trying to get him." My dad explains.

"Get him then!" I yell.

"He's gone." He replies.

I look over to the trees then back at my dad, I shake my head and open the car door and climb in. I continue looking for Killian, he didn't appear. Maybe he's watching my dad to see who his family is so he can kill us next.

We pull up to the hospital. I can't believe how much I have processed today. I know that I will sleep tonight especially since my energy was drained from Quin's voodoo crap.

"Are you ok son? You look ill." My dad asks.

"I'm fine. Today is just catching up on me." I reassure.

"You can leave this visit until tomorrow if you want?" He imposes.

"No! I promised Callie and I never break promises no matter how tired or ill I am." I yell.

"Ok. I'm only thinking about your health Lockie." My dad mutters.

"You should know me by now dad. I'm selfless." I say with a smile.

"Being selfless is a kind thing Lockie but please don't use all your energy on people who don't deserve it. I don't mean Callie when I say that." He explains. I nod and get out of the car.

"Are you walking home or do you want me to pick you up?" He asks.

"I'll walk," I say bluntly then close the door.

I stroll to the hospital entrance and make my way over to the reception desk.

"Which ward is Callie Willis on?" I ask politely.

"Visiting?" The receptionist asks.

"Yes." I quickly reply.

"Ward 4. Just follow the signs there and asks at that reception which room she is in." The receptionist says with a smile. I nod and begin to follow the signs through the corridors. I get into ward 4.

"Excuse me? I'm looking for Callie Willis?" I ask the receptionist.

"Room 6." She answers bluntly.

I roll my eyes and go to look for her room. It doesn't take me long to find her room.

Knock, Knock

"Come in!" Callie shouts.

"Hey! It's me!" I shout then laughs.

"Lync! I'm so happy to see you!" She says excitedly.

"I told you I don't break promises." I smile.

"You're not wrong. Are you ok? You look drained." She asks.

"Been a busy day with appointments and stuff I'm fine," I explain. Suddenly the doctor walks in.

"Hello, Miss Willis. I'm just organizing your medication and file. How are you feeling?" He asks pleasantly.

"I'm fine. More than fine now my best friend is here." She smiles.

The doctor turns to look at me. He gives me an evil look. If looks could kill that would be one of them.

"Got a problem?" I ask him as I fold my arms.

"I do actually." The doctor starts.

"Look. It's got nothing to do with me about your failures so don't get me involved!" I yell.

"You're getting yourself involve Lockie." He says with a creepy smile.

"Lockie?" Callie repeats then looks at me.

"You must have me confused with someone else doctor. Seems like you're the one who needs help." I bark as I try to cover up the truth.

"Why don't we go and talk privately?" The doctor insists.

"Sure but it will be short and sweet since I'm here to visit my friend," I add.

The doctor nods and opens the room door. I walk through the door first.

"I'll be back in a minute Callie," I reassure.

I walk out into the corridor and the doctor closes the door. He leads the way to a private room and I awkwardly follow. We turn to a door and he opens it.

"Guests first." He says as he holds the door open.

I walk into the room and he shuts the door behind us.

"You have no right to reveal who I am!" I scream as I point to him.

"Mr. Saunders. You remind me so much of your brother Killian." He says with a smile.

"Stop it! I'm nothing like him you creep!" I yell.

"Oh have I touched a nerve?" The doctor laughs.

"You're a professional! Well, you're supposed to be. It sounds like to me that you spent too much time obsessing over my brother and his illness." I propose.

"I tried to make him better!" He screams.

"You made him worse!" I scream back.

"He wouldn't be a psychopath/serial killer if you didn't have hold of him. You messed his head up. You pushed him to breaking point!" I continue.

"It has nothing to do with me, Mr. Saunders." He smirks.

"Shut the hell up you creep," I shout as I turn to the door. I try to open it but it's locked.

"What the hell?" I whisper.

"Yes, Mr. Saunders I've locked us in." He laughs.

I turn to look at the doctor and put my hands behind my back and grab my phone. Luckily I have my dad's work phone on speed dial and I can press it without looking. I press it and put it back in my pocket so he can hear the conversation.

"So why have you locked us in?" I start.

"Because you're cocky, know it all brat with a big mouth just like your brother! And I want to show who is the boss here." He shrieks.

"Let me guess... as you did with Killian?" I interrupt.

"I didn't damage your brother! When are you going to get that into your head!" He growls.

"Sounds like you're the one with a screw loose Doc." I chuckle.

"You have the same DNA as your brother Lockie. You can't escape fate." He smiles as he turns to sit at his desk.

"I have no signs of the illness. Killian had signs since he was 12! I'm not an angry person unless you provoke me." I yell.

"We can do blood tests if you like Mr. Saunders. Then I can prove it's in your blood to be a monster like him." He laughs.

Knock, Knock

I smile as I know it will be my dad and his team. What the doctor doesn't know is that they are listening to the conversation and that I have a GPS tracker on my phone. What an idiot.

"Uh, um... Just a moment I'm busy." The doctor answers.

"It's the police open the door." An officer shouts. The doctor looks at me. His face appears to turn redder and redder by the second. I smile and grab my phone from my back pocket. I look at the screen and the call was still going. I turn it around to show the doctor.

"Whoops, my bad," I smirk and shrug.

"Best open that door doc." I laugh.

The doctor rushes over to the door and unlocks it. The police throw the door open and my dad runs over to me.

"Are you ok son? He's not hurt you, has he?" He panics as he checks me over.

"No, dad. His bark is worse than his bite." I laugh.

I walk out of the room and left my dad and his team to deal with Doctor Creep.

I make my way back down the corridor to Callie's room. I knock and walk-in.

"Sorry, but your doctor is a freak." I laugh.

"Why?" She chuckles.

"He went all psycho on me so I had to ring my dad slyly to get him caught," I explain.

"Wow... I noticed he was a bit of a weirdo. More so when he called you Lockie. I thought it was an urban legend?" Callie goes on.

"Yeah... So did I..." I trail off.

Chapter 5

The Beginning of the End

Today is the day I've got to pretend to be the old me. Go on this urban hunt with Trey and Deccan. I'll have to put the idea to them. I head downstairs. I open the living room door. I see my mum and dad are sitting in their usual places. I close the door behind me.

"Are you ok Lockie?" My mum asks.

"Yeah... I'm going out with my friends tonight if that's ok?" I ask.

"What time?" My dad interrupts.

"7 pm," I reply bluntly.

"As long as you come back at the weekend curfew." My mum adds.

"That's 10 pm right?" I ask.

"Yes no later!" My dad booms.

I nod and walk into the kitchen. I grab my skates from the back door. I know Trey and Deccan skateboard so they must be at the park today. I grab my rucksack from the hooks and pack my vans inside.

"What are you rushing about for?" Piper asks as she walks into the kitchen.

"Nothing," I answer.

"You're planning something... I can sense that you're up to no good." Piper snickers.

"It's got nothing to do with you." I splutter.

"Just saying... it's not like you do go behind mum and dad's back. You're the golden child remember?" She laughs.

"Shut up," I growl.

"This is not like you at all. Since you've seen Quin you've changed." Piper shouts.

"Changed good or bad?" I laugh.

"Bad." She says bluntly.

"Oh well, everything has to change at some point." I ramble on.

I quickly tie my skate laces and open the yard door. I climb to my feet slowly whilst holding into the granite kitchen bar and the flimsy door handle.

"Be a jerk all your life then." Piper shrieks as she storms out and slams the kitchen door shut behind her. I couldn't help but smile to myself. I have never got Piper to that point before. Finally, after years of trying, I make her snap by ignoring her.

I get to the skate park and skate over to the ramps. Trey and Deccan are sat chilling at the top with their bikes stood behind them.

"Hey, guys!" I shout.

"We're not in your bad books still are we?" Deccan asks as he glances at Trey and back to me.

"Err... yeah. You left Callie to be in danger and because of your actions she's now recovering in hospital." I argue as I fold my arms.

"Dude, we didn't leave her. We lost her." Trey interrupts as he looks at Deccan.

"We were in Dead Man's Woods when we did the Psycho Dare. Then messed up crap started happening and we all scattered. I found Trey then we looked for Callie and couldn't find her." Deccan explains as he pushes himself up.

"So that explains why she rang me being so upset." I splutter as I look down at the floor.

"It's fine it's over with now." Trey chirps as he jumps to his feet.

"So why have you two not got the Psycho Curse?" I blurt out as I skate into the center of the ramp.

"My dad," Trey says bluntly. He then rides down the ramp on his BMX bike to where I am standing.

"Don't start interrogating me!" Trey continues as he speeds off to the other side of the ramp.

"Deccan?" I ask as I look up at him positioning his bike on the ramp.

"Look, something isn't right with you McCarthy. Your attitude stinks dude." He snaps. He then rolls down the ramp and waits for Trey next to me.

"I'm trying to get to the bottom of this stupid urban hunt thing you've been on." I bark. I then skate to the side of the ramp.

"Look if you want to find out for yourself we can go tonight. Me, you, and Trey. And trust me, you won't last 2 minutes once you have that Psycho Curse McCarthy." Deccan snorts as he swings his leg round from his bike.

"Deal," I smirk.

Trey speeds over and stops with a slide. He pauses and looks at Deccan then back at me.

"OK ladies untangle your knickers. What's going on?" Trey asks followed by a sigh.

"Dead Man's Woods tonight. Me, you, and Deccan. Show me how it was done with Callie." I say with a smile.

Trey climbs from his bike. I skate over to them.

"You McCarthy... are crazy!" Trey yells as he points to me.

"We're all crazy people! Me and you have done it before and we're doing it again!" Deccan shouts to Trey.

I laugh then glance over to the tall church building in the distance. It's only a 15-minute walk to get there.

"Guys. Didn't the legend state that the Saunders remains are in that church graveyard?" I ask as I continue to stare at the church.

"Apparently, why?" Trey asks as he walks over to stand next to me.

"Let's go then," I say as I shuffle my rucksack onto my shoulder properly.

"Let's not!" Deccan yells from behind.

I and Trey turn to look at him. He stands still holding his bike closely next to him as he stares ahead at the church.

"Why not?" Trey questions.

"The reason no one has suggested that is because people believe that's where Killian spends most of his time." He panics as he clenches the handles on his bike.

"Dude. It's an urban legend." Trey replies calmly as he climbs back onto his bike.

"Precisely! LEGEND! Not a Myth." Deccan stutters.

"Man up dude. We're going." Trey grumbles as he nods to me.

"Ok, but if we did tell my family I'm sorry!" Deccan yells as he runs over to us with his bike.

"Dude... how can we tell your family that if we're all dead?" I interrupt.

"You're making my anxiety worse Lync!" He screams.

"No one is going to die, You idiot. Snap out of it and let's go." Trey says bluntly as he pushes his foot from the floor and rides off ahead.

"Come on dude. It will be fun!" I smile as I head off to catch up with Trey.

"Oh ok. If you say so." Deccan stumbles as he follows behind.

We arrive at the cemetery gates. The three of us stare at the gates before us. A sense of fear and anxiety start, which cause adrenaline to kick in. My heart is racing so fast that it feels as if it can explode.

"So, who's going in first?" Trey asks as he climbs from his bike.

"Ha! Not me!" Deccan shouts as he jumps off his bike.

I sit on the floor and begin to untie my skates.

"Lync can go first!" Trey demands as he places his bike up against the wall.

"Sure..." I hesitantly reply as I pull my skates off and place them next to me.

"We will follow behind don't worry," Deccan assures as he puts his bike with Trey's against the wall.

I pull my vans from my rucksack and put my skates inside. I begin putting my vans on and I hear something.

"If you can hear me, I'm so sorry little brother."

I pause. I suddenly get a strange cold feeling rushing through my body.

"Did you hear that?" I ask Trey and Deccan. They both turn to look at me as if I am going crazy.

"Hear what?" Trey asks.

"Never mind," I reply as I tuck my laces into my vans.

"Dude don't do that!" Deccan shouts.

"I only ask if you could hear something. Chill dude. You're like a freaked out cat!" I yell.

I stand to my feet and throw my rucksack onto my right shoulder and shuffle it on properly. Then I take a deep breath then slowly exhale.

"It's now or never boys." I huff as I start to take my first steps towards the gates.

"Too right!" Trey laughs as he follows.

"Yup," Deccan mumbles as he stays back.

I follow the pathway to the back of the cemetery and then see a small walkway through the hedge. I stop and turn to smile at Trey and Deccan.

"It's there isn't it?" Trey whispers, and I nod.

Slowly I approach the walkway in the hedge, poke my head through to see who or what I can see.

"Clear. Come on." I whisper to Trey and Deccan.

We slowly crept through the hedge and stand and stare at the lone gravestone.

"Dude... It's no urban legend. It's freaking real!" Deccan screams.

"Calm down!" Trey shouts to him.

"How can I calm down when the Saunders grave is yards away from us! What the hell man! I thought it was made up!" Deccan continues. I shake my head and begin to approach the gravestone.

"Dude. They're dead." Trey implies.

"They are! Killian isn't!" He continues to scream.

"Guys? Come here..." I shout over.

"As if he has gone over!" Deccan cries.

"Shut up," Trey replies bluntly.

Trey approaches the gravestone and kneels beside me. I watch his eyes closely examine the stone. He is looking up and down and continues to do so.

"Something doesn't feel right." He grumbles as he places his hand onto the stone.

"What do you mean?" I ask.

"He can sense unearthly things. A bit like his dad." Deccan butts in.

"We need to dig this up tonight before Dead Man's Woods." He demands as he stands up.

"Are you crazy?" I yell as I stand up also.

"Yeah, a little. But I feel something isn't right." He adds as he scratches his head.

I glance over at the trees and see a hooded figure watching us. My entire body freezes.

"Err..." I splutter.

"What?" Deccan asks as he turns in the direction I am facing.

"It's him!" He screams as he begins to run to the hedge.

"We need to go Lync! Now!" Trey demands as he grips my arm.

"It's... It's... Him..." I stutter.

"Dude let's not wait for him to come to us yeah? Run!" He screams.

The fear rushes through my veins. I freeze because of past events I've faced with Killian. I can't face him, I'm not as brave as I thought I was. I run with Trey and Deccan. We ran until we finally felt safe. We get to the cemetery gates. I'm hoping we are safe. I stop. I have to look back to see if Killian is still following us.

"Lync! Are you crazy?" Deccan screams as he grips his bike.

"Maybe I am. If he isn't following us I want to go back." I suggest as I stare into the cemetery.

"Dude. It's not freaking safe!" Trey yells as he climbs onto his bike.

"Well if you two aren't coming with me, I'm going on my own." I impose as I slowly walk towards the cemetery once more.

Trey grabs my hoodie from behind.

"We do this together or not at all." He reassures.

"Why?" I ask as I push his hand from my hoodie.

"You're like a brother to us now man, we won't allow you to do anything stupid alone. Even if you want to chat up a girl we're there. We're bros." He says calmly.

I glance over to Deccan. He looks how I feel, pale, shaky scared.

"Let's just do whatever for now. Calm ourselves down from this near miss then come back later to check the remains." I insist.

"Sounds good." Trey smiles then heads to Deccan who is sitting on his bike a few yards away.

We begin to head back to the skate park to see if it will help calm our nerves. I couldn't believe that Killian almost had us. That won't be happening again.

I sit under the shelter at the skate park. I grab Trey's cigarettes and flip the packet open. I take a cigarette out, then I reach over for his Zippo lighter. I light it and lie down on the floor. I take my time to inhale the smoke, then slowly exhale. I turn the cigarette to look at it above me.

"My parents would kill me if they found out," I mumble to myself as I put the cigarette back to my lips.

"Lync!" Trey shouts as he speeds over on his bike.

"What?" I answer quickly as I turn to face his direction.

"It's not like you to have a smoke. What's up?" He asks worryingly as he pulls up next to the shelter.

"Just trying everything to calm myself dude, that's all," I reply as I put the cigarette back to my lips for another toke.

"You don't want to get into that habit dude unless you want to. It's hard to stop." He explains.

"To be an honest man... I don't care at this moment in time." I reply bluntly as I flicked the ash from the cigarette.

"Ok dude. Your choice." He grumbles.

I turn to look back up at the ceiling of the shelter. To come to think of it I have a lot of issues at the moment. I've almost lost a friend, found out that I'm Lockie, Killian the psychopath is my brother, I'm adopted, my parents were murdered and worst of all I've almost been caught by Killian. So I feel I deserve to start smoking.

"Hey, guys!" A voice shouts from a few yards away. I quickly throw myself up to sit up.

"Callie!" I shout as I flicked my cigarette into the grass and quickly blew out the smoke from my lungs.

"You smoke?" She asks sternly.

"Today he's started." Trey butts in.

"I leave you with him and you get him into your dirty habits." She growls as she walks towards Trey.

"It's got nothing to do with Trey. I'm going through a lot of stuff at the moment." I stress as I stand up.

"We're here if you need to talk Lync," Callie assures me.

"I don't want to talk about it, to be honest," I mumble as I walk towards the ramps where Deccan is. I glance over as I walk away and see that Callie and Trey are talking and looking over to me. I turn back to get to Deccan and shake my head.

"Yo Deccan!" I shout to grab his attention. He turns to look at me and rides over.

"Can you do me a favor bro?" I ask as I put my hands into my pockets.

"Yeah, sure!" He smiles.

"If I give you the money, could you get some cigarettes for me from the shop?" I ask with a smile.

"Sure bro." He replies as he holds his hand out.

"Thanks, man." I hand him my money. Deccan then heads off to the shop and I make my way back to Trey and Callie.

"Don't do anything stupid." Callie scolds as she points to me.

"You're not my mother Callie," I mumble as I head to the shelter again.

I sit down then lay back down on my back. I begin to think of a plan for later with Killian.

Chapter 6

The Time is Now

I approach the front gates of my house. Trey and Deccan are waiting at the end of the street for me. I open the gate and close it quietly behind me. I enter the house and pull my skates out of my bag and place them in the hall. As I zip my rucksack up my dad opens the living room door.

"We didn't hear you come in through the door son. Are you ok?" My dad asks as he leans onto the frame of the door.

"Yeah, I'm alright. Just going back out with Trey and Deccan. I will be home for 10." I reply with a slight smile.

"No worries son. Be careful! If you need me to pick you up call me." My dad says in a fathering tone.

"Sure," I answer bluntly as I walk out of the door.

I open the gate and jog down the street to Trey and Deccan. I feel excited to do this but nervous and scared at the same time. I can't believe I've said for us to go ahead with Dead Man's Woods, I'm so stupid.

"Right bro. We ready?" Trey asks with a smile. I nod and jump onto the pegs at the back of his bike. We head off down the road towards Dead Man's Woods.

It's starts to become dark and we have just arrived at Dead Man's Woods. The worst part is... there is no plan. The only plan we have is to come here and do the psycho dare and gain the psycho's curse. Trey and Deccan haven't experienced it properly as Quin got rid of theirs. So we are all nervous and we don't know what to expect.

"I think I've changed my mind." Deccan gulps.

"We do this together or not at all!" Trey reminds us.

I place my hand into my pocket and grab my cigarettes and lighter. I pull one out and put it to my lips and lit it.

"Right Lync? We do this together?" Trey asks with a smile.

"Yeah, man. Together or never." I reply.

We stand and stare towards the trees. I hate the feeling of fear and adrenaline; this is what causes me to freeze. I force myself to walk towards the woods. My body becomes tense.

"We can do this!" Deccan shouts as he follows behind me.

We get to the entrance of the woods. I stop. I couldn't bring myself to do it. My heart feels as if it is going to burst.

"Come on dude! We can do it. We're together, we'll be fine." Trey reassures as he continues towards the woods.

"I guess so..." I splutter as I drop my cigarette onto the floor and step on it.

I grab my phone from my jeans pocket and turn on the flashlight. I look over at Deccan, he has his camera recording with the flashlight on. I quickly turn to Trey, he had his dad's large flashlight.

"Let's make our way to the clearance. That should be the best place to do it." Trey explains as he walks in front of us.

"This will be awesome if I catch it on video!" Deccan chirps as he follows Trey closely.

I took a deep breath and slowly exhale. Just to keep me in check. I follow behind Trey and Deccan, not too close but close enough if anything bad was to happen.

"We're here guys," Trey announces as he places his rucksack onto the dry, dusty dirt below.

He begins to unzip his bag and pulls out an Ouija board. I and Deccan stand and watch in shock.

"Feck off man! I'm not touching that thing!" Deccan yells as he steps back.

"We have to!" Trey argues back as he places it onto the floor.

"I hope you're joking? They're dangerous!" I shout.

"We need to do it properly this time. We need to get the curse fully." Trey explains as he set it up.

I sigh, walk over, and sit in front of the board. I and Trey look over to Deccan who stands staring at us as well as recording.

"I'll just be the cameraman. You guys go ahead." He slurs.

"Sit your ass down!" Trey shrieks.

Deccan shuffles over to us and slowly sits next to me and Trey. Trey looks at us both then smiles.

"Swallow that fear because the weakest gets the curse 100x worse." He smirks as he places his index finger and middle finger onto the planchette.

Again I breathe in then breathe out. I slowly place my index finger and middle finger onto the planchette. I and Trey look to Deccan.

"Ok! I'll do it!" He huffs as he places his fingers onto the planchette.

"Right you two close your eyes. Do not open then until I stop saying the ritual." Trey orders.

I look to Deccan and he nods to me. We turn to face Trey and close our eyes.

"Psycho, psycho where are you? Hiding in the trees or within the leaves. Psycho, psycho where is your brother? Is he with you or is he dead? Psycho, psycho show yourself. If you can't give us a sign." Trey chanted.

I and Deccan quickly open our eyes. I being to breathe rapidly. It feels as if I can't get my breath.

"Whatever you do, DO NOT TAKE YOUR FINGERS OFF!" Trey warns.

I feel weird all of a sudden. Then it clicks... The dare chant mentioned me. That's why it's affecting me!

"I can't do this. I don't feel right." I stutter as I begin to sweat.

"Lync! Don't let go!" Deccan yells.

Suddenly the pancetta moves to 'H' then to 'I' then back to the blank part of the board.

"What the hell man! Not funny!" Trey yells to Deccan.

"It wasn't me; You absolute buffoon!" Deccan screams back.

"Guys..." I say as I stare ahead at the tree.

"What!" Trey and Deccan shout.

"We have a visitor and we can't move!" I point out.

Trey and Deccan look in the direction I am looking in. He is there and he is real.

"God damn it!" Trey yells. "Say goodbye! Say it!" Trey continues yelling.

Killian began to walk towards us. We all go into panic mode and scatter. We can't sit there and says bye to a dead person! We have a serial killer hunting us! I run to a tree and hide behind it. I couldn't help but cry. I've messed up again and this time I will be dead.

"Get. A. Grip!" I whisper to myself as I slap my head.

"Lync... I know where you're hiding." A creepy voice says followed by an insane laugh.

'This can't be possible!' I think whilst tears ran down my cheeks. I slowly place my hand over my mouth.

"You can't hide from me! Nor can you run!" He growls followed by the sound of a knife scraping around the tree. I have no choice but to run.

I quickly push myself from the tree and run towards the path.

"Run, run little boy. I will follow, I will follow you forever!" He screams as he quickly follows behind me.

"Trey! Deccan!" I scream as I continue running.

"They'll not hear your screams Lync. They're gone!" He laughs.

I cry more. I have never felt so petrified in my whole life! I never knew what the word fully meant until now. I got to the path and follow it to the entrance. I check behind me and Killian keeps running. He can catch me at any moment. His face, I can never forget what he did to himself. Whiteface and Chelsea Grin. It can't get any creepier than it already is. I get out of Dead Man's Woods and Trey and Deccan are waiting for me.

"Go! Go! Just go!" I scream as my voice cracks multiple times.

Trey and Deccan jump onto their bikes ready to ride off. I quickly get to Trey and jump on his pegs, he speeds off. I look behind and see Killian waving with his scary smile and his knife in his hand. What has he become? That is not my brother... that is a monster.

We get to the skate park. I jump off the back of Trey's bike and collapse onto the floor onto my hands and knees.

"What the hell!" Trey yells.

I continue to cry. I scream and scream then grip my hair and put my head onto the floor.

"Lync? What happened in there?" Deccan asks worryingly.

I shake my head then begin to head-butt the floor. I can feel the psycho curse taking over. My head is burning, ears are ringing.

"He almost had me." I sob whilst my face was still on the floor.

"That was a close call dude. We shouldn't have split!" Deccan barks.

"We had no choice idiot!" Trey yells.

"He's got the curse a hell of a lot worse than us!" Deccan snaps.

"Shut up," I mumble.

"If it wasn't for you freaking out we would have had a chance to fix this!" Trey scolds.

"Shut... up," I growl.

"Don't blame this on me you prick! You're the one with the Ouija board!" Deccan spits.

"SHUT THE HELL UP!" I shriek as I sat up. Trey and Deccan look at me.

"It was my fault. My idea. Now shut up." I growl as I slowly stood up. I shuffle my rucksack onto my back. I begin to head home.

Chapter 7

Sweet Dreams

10.03 pm. Just three minutes after my curfew. I sneak through the front door of my house. Quietly I place my rucksack onto the floor. I begin to tiptoe up the stairs making sure I don't make any sound to grab my parent's attention. Then the living room door opens.

"You're late." My mum says calmly. I freeze on the stairs.

"Err... A few minutes maybe?" I reply as I scrunch my face to prepare for her to tell me off.

"You're always 5 minutes early. Always. Where have you been?" She asks. I slowly turn to face her.

"Just the skate park," I reply nervously.

"Well, that's a lie right there. What's got into you?" She growls as she folded her arms. I sit on the step below my feet.

"I was just out," I reply hesitantly.

"Kevin!" My mum screams.

I hear the kitchen door fling open and heavy footsteps heading towards the living room door. My heart begins to race. I can't tell them what I've been up to! Suddenly the living room door is pulled open. My dad's facial expression shows how much trouble I'm in.

"Where have you been?" He bellows.

"I've just been out with Trey and Deccan. Why do I have to tell you the specifics?" I yell as I stand up.

Before I can even react my mum reaches over and slaps me across my face. I pause in shock.

"How dare you speak to us like that!" She cries.

I slowly turn to my mum and dad with my head down. My hair covering my face. I put my hand onto my cheek where my mum has smacked me. All the time I have lived with them this has never happened.

"What the hell has got into you Lockie? You've never behaved like this!" My dad yells.

I stand in silence. I move my hand from my face and turn to head upstairs. As I am about to take my first step my dad grabs my hoodie.

"Don't you walk away from us when we are speaking to you!" He shouts.

I turn to him and push his hand from my hoodie and ran upstairs before he had the chance to grab me again. I reach for my door handle when Piper appears out of her room.

"In here! I have a lock on my door." She whispers as she gestured to go over to her. I quickly ran over to her room and she shut the door and locked it behind her.

"So what's with you becoming the black sheep?" She asks followed with a smirk as she walks towards me.

"I'm not becoming a black sheep. I was a few minutes late for my curfew." I explain as I hold my head down.

"Sure. You're doing a lot of sneaking Lockie, it won't be long until you get caught." She huffs as she sits on the bed.

"I don't care," I grumble as I stumble to her bedroom door.

"Suit yourself. Take a leaf out of this black sheep's book." She laughs.

I shake my head and unlock the door. It's a big mistake following Piper into her room. She has always been the rebel in the family. I open the door and head towards my bedroom. I push my door open and look around. Everything was how I left it. I close the door behind me and walk over to my wardrobe to get changed. Suddenly I get a stinging pain on the top of my back.

"What the hell?" I mumble as I turn my back to the mirror.

I slowly lift my t-shirt until I got to the part of my back that is stinging. At this point, I had to grit my teeth and peel my t-shirt from my back. The pain was excruciating! I scream as I peel my shirt off slowly. My eyes begin to fill with tears.

"I can't do this!" I cry as my t-shirt was halfway off my back.

Suddenly I have a thought. Maybe it will be easier if I just rip it off like a band-aid. I did exactly that. I fell to the floor in pain. I cry as I try to hold in the screams.

"What even is it!" I yell as I stand up to look in the mirror.

A burn across the top of my back. It wasn't just a burn. It was writing. I walk back towards the mirror to read it.

LET'S PLAY PSYCHO

I turn to face the mirror. I can't be seeing things. This is 100% real! The pain and the way it looks. It's all real.

Knock, knock

"Don't come in!" I scream as I run around my bedroom to try and hide my back.

It was too late. My dad opens the door.

"Lockie! What the hell is going on?" He yells as he walks in.

"Nothing." I splutter as I quickly wipe the tears from my face.

"Turn around." He asks calmly.

"I can't." I sniffle as I hold my back against the wall.

"I said turn around!" My dad booms as he walks towards me.

"No! Please don't! Don't!" I scream as he grabs my arm.

"What on earth is going on?" My mum asks as she walks in.

My dad quickly swings me around so he can look at my back. He and my mum are silent.

"See! I told you not to! It freaks and hurts like hell!" I cry as I turn to face them.

"Lockie... there's nothing here sweetheart." My mum answers.

"What?" I ask as I run over to my mirror again.

"There's nothing there, son!" My dad yells.

I turn my back to the mirror and turn to look. The whole thing has gone. I glance over to my t-shirt that was covered in blood and bits of skin, it was clean.

"Sorry... I must be imagining things." I answer calmly as I climb into bed.

My dad shakes his head and walks out of the room. My mum watches him as he leaves then comes over to my bed. She sat on the edge and begins to stroke my hair.

"If you ever need to speak to us don't be afraid to." She whispers as she tucks my hair behind my ear.

"I'm fine, mum," I whisper back.

"I know you're not. So when you are ready to talk you know where I am." She reassures as she stands up.

"I'll be fine," I reply with a slight smile.

My mum nods then makes her way out of my bedroom. She shuts the door behind her which then leaves me in a room of silence.

I awake. Well, I think I have. My room is dark, so dark that I can't make out some of the items and objects in my room. I sit up and rub my eyes. I take another look around to allow my eyes to adjust to the darkness. Suddenly my bed covers begin to move. I jump out of bed and run over to my wardrobe. I watch my bed covers in fear. Then suddenly they stop moving. I breathe a sigh of relief. Out of nowhere, the bed covers began to lift as if someone's in the bed. It wasn't long until I notice a figure form in the covers.

"Mum! Dad! Piper! Anyone!" I scream as loud as I possibly could.

"They can't hear you." A creepy voice replies followed by a scarily insane laugh.

"This can't be real. This cannot be real!" I panic as I slowly reverse into my wardrobe.

"Yes, Lync it's your worse nightmare!" The figure growls as he reveals himself.

"Killian! You don't even know where I live!" I yell.

"You're right. That's why I start by turning your sweet dreams into nightmares!" He smirks as he steps from the bed.

Then he lunges himself towards me and pins me to the wardrobe. He raises his knife to my throat.

"Go on scream!" He laughs.

I begins to scream and try everything to get him off me. I push, kick, and push myself from the wardrobe to try and break free. Nothing is working.

"WAKE UP LOCKIE!" A voice screams.

I awake to see my mum who looks horrified, my dad who sitting on my bed, and Piper who also looks scared at the door.

"What happened?" I ask as I sit up and rub my eyes.

"You had a night terror. You haven't had one of those since before Quin wiped your memory." My dad explains.

"But if it was just a night terror why are you all looking scared?" I question as I glance around at everyone.

"It wasn't a normal one sweetheart, you looked as if you were having a seizure followed by a blood-curdling scream." My mum adds.

"Explains the headache," I grumble as I place my hand onto my head.

"Anyway go back to sleep son. It's 3 am." My dad suggests as he stands up.

"I'm not promising I'll go back to sleep after that experience." I splutter as I lay back down.

"Night." My mum says sweetly as she waits to close the door.

"Goodnight son." My dad says with a smile as he walks out of the bedroom. My mum closes the door behind him.

There's no way I'm going back to sleep.

Chapter 8

I Can't Handle It!

I get out of bed. I haven't slept since the night terror at 3 am. I reach for my phone from the top of the drawers and unlock it. I quickly scroll through my contacts for Trey's number. I finally find it and call him. He answers straight away.

"Lync! Did anything happen last night?" He panics.

"Yeah man, I had a severe night terror. I've not had one since I was 13. What about you?" I ask as I yawn.

"Dude, I had freakin sleep paralysis! Guess who it was crushing me?" Trey yells.

"Killian?" I answer.

"Yeah! I didn't know if he was there or not! I don't think I can sleep now." He shouts.

"Yeah... I don't think I can do this anymore man." I mumble.

"We need to! We need answers Lync." He continues.

"Dude, what if he pulls the Freddie Kruger stunt and kills us in our sleep? We wouldn't be able to do anything!" I scream.

"From what I know it's not possible. Freddie Kruger is fictional, this is real." He explains.

"Ok well, meet me at the skate park in half an hour. We can talk properly there." I propose.

"Sure see you then man," Trey says as he hangs up.

I place my phone back on top of my drawers. I open the top drawer and grab my black denim shorts. I then walk over to my wardrobe and grab my grey slogan t-shirt. It reads 'Parental Advisory Explicit Content' it's one of my favourite t-shirts. I begin to get dressed.

"Lync. I have a surprise for you." A voice whispers.

I quickly turn and look around my bedroom no one was there. I shook my head and continue to get dressed.

"Don't act like you can't hear me!" The voice growls.

I finish getting my shorts on and look around again. I don't want to look stupid talking to something that's not there.

"Want me to show you something?" The voice continues.

"You're not real! Go away!" I yell as I ran over to my shoe rail.

I quickly drag my DC sneakers from the rail and go to open my bedroom door. It's jammed.

"What the hell?" I mumble to myself.

I hop around to get my DC's on as quickly as I can.

"Behind you." A woman's voice whispers.

I pause and I manage to get my sneakers on. But I freeze because I had a sense of presence behind me. My hairs on my body all stood on end. I swallow, I close my eyes and turn around.

"OPEN YOUR EYES!" A male voice shrieks.

My eyes open to see a figure stood behind me. Their head was down and they were wearing a black hoodie. I couldn't see their face because of the hood. Their hands were perfectly sat inside the hoodie pockets. My eyes look down, he is wearing black skinny jeans and black converse. I slowly walk back to the door as my eyes look back up to his face which was still not physically visible. It's clear... it's Killian.

"What do you want from me?" I ask as I could feel the fear building.

Killian lifts his head slightly. His Chelsea Grin shows and he smiles.

"I want you." He laughs.

"Dad! Mum!" I cry as I turn to the door once more to attempt to open it.

"You can't leave." Killian chuckles.

I grab the door handle tight and began to shake the door. I heard my dad running upstairs.

"Dad! Help me please!" I scream in fear.

I turn to look where Killian is standing to plan how I can get past him. I make a run to his right, he instantly grabs me. My dad tries to open the door.

"Get off me!" I yell as I struggle to break free from his grip.

"I'll kick the door! Stand back!" My dad shouts from behind the door.

Killian pulls me towards him and put his arm around my throat. He pulls his knife out with his free hand.

"Dad hurry!" I scream.

My dad kicks the door and it flew open. He stands and looks at me. I also stand and look at him back, like nothing has happened.

"What the hell was all the screaming?" He shrieks as he folds his arms.

"Long story," I mumble as I push past him in the doorway and run towards the stairs.

I get downstairs and grab my rucksack. As I reach for the front door my mum opens the living room door and my dad walks towards me on the stairs.

"What's going on Lockie? You're not yourself." My mum asks in a concerned tone.

"Just not been able to shake off the night terror last night that's all," I reply as I put my rucksack over my shoulders.

"Has anything happened that we need to know about? You haven't had a night terror since you were 13 sons." My dad asks as he leans onto the stair rail.

"Nope. Everything is ok." I say with a smile as I pull open the front door.

"You would tell us if anything happened wouldn't you?" My mum asks. I stop on the pathway towards the gate.

"Yes, mum I would," I reply bluntly and continue to the gate.

I leave my safe zone, my home. Even though he knows where I am and he can haunt me there, my parents are there when I need them.

I arrive at the main gates of the park. I grab my phone from my back pocket and press the lock button. The time flashes up at 9.02 am. I put my phone back in my pocket. I look down the road to my right then look to my left. There is no sign of Trey. Then I hear voices from the trees behind me.

"So it's just $10?" A voice asks.

"Shhh. Yeah dude, unless you want more and I can do it for $20." Another voice reply.

"Thanks. Here."

I walk over, they're dealing here. If it's something that can help me get out of this hell after being cursed I'm going to take my chances.

"Hey. What are you selling?" I ask nervously.

"Don't! He will probably get you in the nick!" The guy warns.

"No... I'm having a rough time. I need something to keep me going." I explain.

"The best thing for that would be whizz," The dealer reply.

"$20 worth then please," I add.

He nods and reaches into his inside pocket. He grabs a bag of white powder and gave it to me. I gave him $20 in exchange. I hand him my number and proceed to go to the main gates and wait for Trey. Instead, Trey is already there waiting for me.

"Hey man! I've been looking for you." I laugh as I approach him.

"I was wondering where you were. Why have you come from that direction?" Trey asks as he walks towards me.

"As I've just said... I was looking for you." I reply.

Trey stands in front of me and looks at me up and down. He went silent like he knew I was up to something.

"Na, I don't buy it. Your whole demeanour tells me something is off." Trey says as he walks past me and pushes my shoulder with his.

"Dude! Last night was messed up! Bear with me." I yell as I run over to catch up with him.

"And you don't think it wasn't for me?" Trey snaps.

I went silent. I didn't want to argue over what he believes. This is all my fault. I've drag Trey and Deccan into this mess. They don't deserve to withstand this trauma.

"I'm sorry man. I shouldn't have got you and Deccan to do that stupid dare!" I say as I drag my feet.

Trey stops and turns to face me. I can see the fear in his eyes. The fear which I caused as I was too selfish to drag my friends down with me. Too scared to do it alone.

"If we die, who's to blame?" He grumbles.

I look to the floor in shame and disgust. How to turn your friends against you instantly?

"If anything happens to you or Deccan I'll take the blame. It is my fault after all." I splutter.

I look up and Trey shakes his head and continues towards the skate park as I follow.

The guilt is taking over. The fear of falling asleep and seeing Killian again began to creep up on me. I look at Trey; he is slouched on the wall waiting for Deccan. I slip my hand inside my pocket. I grab my house key and the bag I got from the guy. I glance back over to Trey who was still not taking notice. I turn my back and open the bag. I place the end of my key inside and collected a small pile of white powder at the end. I slowly pull it out. I put it to my nose and sniff until it was gone. I quickly put the bag and key in my pocket. I sniff twice then rub my nose.

"You ok man?" Trey asks from behind.

"Yeah. Just feel guilty." I sniff.

"Don't. We all agreed to do it together. I'm sorry for taking it out on you." He explains followed with a smile.

I nod and head over to the shelter and sit down. Even though Trey apologized but I still feel bad. Trey sits down next to me.

"I can't do this anymore," I say as I begin to cry.

"Do what?" Trey asks.

"This curse thing! I feel like I'm going insane." I cry.

"That's what the curse does Lync. We all knew this." Trey explains.

"I didn't realize how bad it was." I sniffle.

"It's not at it's worst yet Lync, it's the beginning of it," Trey admitted.

Suddenly I felt the effects of the drug kick in. My heart begins to race; my breathing becomes faster. But the feeling is intense but yet amazing and I felt awake with a sudden rush of energy.

I stand up and head over to the trees across from where I and Trey are sitting.

"Dude where you going? You're acting strange." Trey says as he stands up.

"I want to be alone for a minute," I reply.

As I get to the trees to I sit down, then a weird feeling comes over me. I begin to chuckle to myself and I can't control it. I look up and see Killian in the distance. I smile at him though I didn't feel like myself. I felt as if I was losing grip with reality... but I like it.

"Join me Lync." A voice says.

It sounds clear like the person is next to me. I laugh and close my eyes.

"I can't. I'm not like you." I reply.

I know that it's Killian. These drugs are making me weak for him to connect with me. But I need it to stop the night terrors.

"You and I are the same Lync, I was like you once. Let me help you." He whispers.

"I can't do what you do," I add followed by a smirk.

"You will eventually." He replies.

Then it goes silent. I look to my left and see Callie standing there staring at me in disbelief.

"What the hell?" She snaps. I quickly stand up.

"How long have you been there?" I ask.

"Long enough..." She says as she steps back slowly.

"Look Callie, you're not thinking straight after the hospital. You didn't see anything. I was just sat here." I snap.

"Lync... you sounded like you had lost it..." She says.

"I've not Callie! I'm me!" I continue to persuade her.

"The Lync I knew was sweet and caring... the person in front of me reminds me of Killian from the Urban Legend..." She replies.

"I'm nothing like him! Don't you ever compare me with a psychotic lunatic!" I yell.

Trey then runs over to us with Deccan. They look at us confused.

"What's going on?" Trey asks.

"Lync has lost it. He sounds like a psychopath." Callie says as she stands next to him.

"She's lying! I was just sat there!" I scream.

"Dude... you've been acting weird since we met up. What's going on with you?" Trey asks.

"I'm fine!" I snap as I stand up.

"Trey? His pupils are dilated. He's either high or officially lost it." Deccan adds.

"Fuck you all," I growl as I head to the skate park exit.

Chapter 9

What's Happening To Me?

I get home and quickly shut the front door. I run upstairs towards my bedroom.

"Lockie, is that you?" My mum shouts.

"Yeah, I'm going upstairs!" I shout back.

I get to the top of the stairs and Piper is standing on the landing. She walks over to me and looks me dead in the eyes.

"Are you... high?" She smirks.

"No!" I snap as I push her aside.

"Oh my god. Yes, you are! Holy crap. You are so becoming a rebel." She continues.

"Shut up!" I growl.

I quickly get into my bedroom and close the door. I then sit in front of the door to make sure no one enters. I pull my key and bag out of my pocket. I untie the bag and put the end of the key in again. I collect another small pile of white powder at the end of the key and carefully pull it out. Quickly I sniff it until it disappears. I tie the bag again and put it in my pocket along with my key. I close my eyes.

"You're back again I see," Killian says followed by a chuckle.

I smile and slouched onto my door. I feel the rush I was hoping for again.

"Yes, I'm home." I smile.

"I want you to join me." He begs.

"I can't," I reply.

The way I'm feeling was beginning to scare me but the feeling I was experiencing seems similar to what I had read about Killian and what he experienced. It feels great! I begin to laugh uncontrollably. I stand and place my hands on my face and began to pace my bedroom.

"What's happening to me!" I growl.

"You're starting to feel what I felt!" Killian laughs.

"I'm not you!" I yell.

I begin to try and fight back to reality. If I continue to take this stuff I'll become a monster like Killian. Unless the doctor creep was right... I could have the same condition as Killian just not showing signs. Until now. Suddenly my phone rings.

"I know your heads messed up at the moment but we've just spoken to the graveyard keeper. Lockie is dead. He is buried with the Saunders." Trey explains.

"Huh? We all know that." I reply. My heart begins to race. They're going to find out I'm not there.

"I know. I, Deccan, and Callie are going to dig it up today. If he is there or not, we need to search for the truth." Trey demands.

"I can help," I add hoping to steer them away from the idea.

"No. You're still high, dude... In the time I've known you Lync I never expected you to take drugs." Trey says disappointingly.

"Well wait a few hours! I won't take it anymore. I'll meet you at the skate park." I splutter.

"Why do you want to do this so bad dude? At first, you were against it." Trey asks.

"I want to get to the bottom of it as much as everyone else," I explain.

I don't want them to get the true information. I can't let them find out the truth. I can't let them find out about me.

"Meet us now and we will wait until you have your come down." Trey insists.

"Yeah sure," I reply.

"Leave your stuff at home. No more." Trey demanded.

"Yes, boss." I laugh.

Trey hangs up and I throw my phone onto my bed. I felt like my friends were turning against me. I felt the rage building.

"Why am I being spoken to like a child?" I yell as I kick my bed.

"Because they don't care Lync." Killian reply.

"I felt like they did care until the curse happened." I continue.

"They play on it. They pretend." Killian laughs.

"Show yourself anyway! Not you know how you were!" I scream.

Suddenly Killian appears, leaning on my wardrobe with his arm. He looked like how I remember him. Brown hair, black hoodie, black skinny jeans, and black converse. I look like him, how he was.

"Wow..." I gasp.

"What?" He asks.

"Why are you acting normal?" I ask.

"Because that's what you wanted." He says with a smile.

"But you're a psychopath! You can't just change." I yell.

"You're right... but there's a connection with you. Like I know you. That's why it's happened." He smirks.

Crap. I must be going loopy. It can't be him. He can't be real.

"You don't know me." I spat.

Killian chuckles and walks towards me. He grabs my arm and pulls me to sit on the bed. He looks me in the eyes.

"There is something..." He replies.

"You... you... just..." I stutter.

"Touched you? Pulled you? Because I'm real." He smiles.

I can't help but look at him in shock. He is really in front of me. But how? How can he change and just appear?

"Lockie! Are you going to be home for dinner?" My mum shouts to me.

I quickly turn to the door then slowly look at Killian. His face looks surprised.

"No, save me some in the oven!" I shout back as I kept my eye on Killian.

"No. This can't be possible!" Killian yells as he stood up from the bed as he continues to look at me in shock.

"Well, the cats out the bag..." I mumble.

"I could never forgive myself! I thought I killed you! You're alive!" Killian laughs.

"You still attempted it," I growl.

"I wasn't thinking!" He continues.

I stand up and head to my desk. I open the drawer with my photo album. I pull out the photo album and hold it out for Killian. He grabs it from my hand and began to flick through the photos.

"It's you! It is my little bro..." He cries.

"So are you going to attempt to kill me again?" I ask.

"No. I feel like how I should be around you." He explains.

"Well stop killing. Stop everything!" I yell.

"I'll try." He says with a smile.

"Anyway, I'm going to have to go and meet my friends. You will have to disappear." I say as I walk to the door. I turn to look at Killian and he was gone. Just like that.

I arrive at the skate park. Trey, Deccan, and Callie were there. As I begin to walk over to them Killian appears in front of me. Immediately I jump up.

"Hey! Don't freakin do that!" I whisper.

"Don't do it!" He begs.

"Don't do what?" I ask as I look at Killian confused.

"Dig up the grave!" He yells.

"It's fine..." I smile as I walk past him.

"No!" He shouts.

I run over to everyone at the shelter in the skate park. I don't understand how Killian keeps appearing and disappearing.

"You made it," Deccan says excitedly.

"Yeah, man," I mumble.

"How are you feeling?" Trey asks.

"A bit on the rubbish side to be honest." I splutter.

Callie begins to look at me up and down in disgust. I turn around and look at the floor whilst slowly pushing the dry dusty mud around with my foot.

"I think we should go and do it now," Deccan suggests.

"We could... no one knows it's there or dares to go near it, to be honest." Trey replies.

"Let's go then," Callie says with a smile.

Everyone begins to head to the exit. I stay back and follow them.

"You don't want to see what's in that grave Lockie!" Killian yelled.

"Just shut up will you," I whisper.

We got to the bushes in the cemetery, and everyone stops. Trey begins to grab the shovels from underneath the bushes.

"Lync you ready bro?" Deccan asks.

I nod and walk past them to the opening in the bushes. I take a deep breath and walk through.

I look around no one was there but me and everyone behind. The grave stands alone.

"You guys ready?" I ask.

"Yeah, dude." Trey replies as he walks past me with the shovels.

Trey passes one to Deccan and keeps one for himself. Callie stands near the grave and watches. I find my way over to her and stand next to her. Trey and Deccan begin to dig.

"I'm sorry about before. I wasn't losing it I was high." I explain.

"It's fine." She snaps.

"I just wanted to clear it up. I don't want to lose our friendship over this." I say as I open my arms to her.

Callie turns and looks at me. Soon enough she smiles and hugs me. We continue to watch Deccan and Trey dig the grave. All of a sudden feel sick and become lightheaded.

"Lync are you ok?" Callie asks.

"Yeah... I just feel a bit off." I answer.

Soon enough Trey hits something with his shovel. He and Deccan immediately look at each other.

"Well... this is a shallow grave," Deccan mumbles.

"Come on let's look," Trey shouts.

Me and Callie slowly walk over. Trey begins digging with his hands. Deccan did also.

"Jackpot. Lockie Saunders." Deccan smiles.

"That was a lucky guess to dig here dude," Trey says as he wiped the golden plaque.

I grab the shovel and pass it to Trey. Then I slowly step back with Callie.

"What are you giving us this for?" Trey asks.

"Open it," I say.

Everyone looks at me in shock.

"Dude, this is proof he is here. We don't need to." Trey splutter.

"Do it," I demand.

Trey throws the shovel to me. It lands in front of my feet. I look down at it then look back at Trey.

"You do it." He says.

"Fine," I yell as I pick up the shovel.

I walk over and jump into the hole with Trey and Deccan. They both step back. I wedge the shovel into the casket door and jump to put all my weight onto the shovel. Suddenly there is a crack.

"I can't believe you're doing this Lync! Just leave the poor boy to rest!" Callie screams.

I continue to push the shovel to open it up, then it opens. I quickly throw the shovel to the side and pull the door. There's nothing there, no one in there.

"What the hell?" Deccan yells.

"He's not there. Now you have your proof." I grumble as I climb out of the hole immediately.

"How is this possible?" Callie asks.

"Does this mean he isn't dead?" Deccan asks.

"All of you shut up!" Trey screams.

I stand next to Callie again and Trey stands and stares into the empty casket. Deccan climbs out and walks over to me and Callie. We watch Trey as he stares at the empty casket. I go over and offer him my hand.

"Come on let's do the research," I say with a smile.

Trey turns to me and nods he grab my hand and I help him out. Then something weird happen as his eyes roll back to the whites of his eyes. His hand is still locked onto mine. I feel his energy and mine connect.

"What's going on!" Callie cries.

"Deccan! Get him off me!" I yell.

Deccan runs over and pulls Trey from me. Trey suddenly flops to the floor.

"Oh my god! Trey!" Callie screams as she runs over.

I stand in shock and freeze because I don't know what has just happened. Trey begins to grumble and sits up holding his head.

"Dude, you ok?" Deccan asks.

Trey turns to look at me. He quickly stands up and power walks towards me.

"Trey! Stop!" Callie yells.

I hold my hands up and he grips my hoodie near my throat and push me into the tree behind.

"You deceiving, vile, liar!" He screams into my face.

"Trey... I don't know what you saw but I can explain." I reassure.

"Explain? Are you joking?" He continues.

Deccan and Callie run over. Deccan grabs Trey and Trey pushes him away with his free hand.

"What's happening?" Callie cries.

"Tell them! Tell them the truth and nothing but the truth!" Trey yells.

I look over to Callie then Deccan who was on the floor. Tears begin to build up.

"I'm... sorry..." I stutter.

"Sorry for what Lync?" Callie asks.

"Don't call him that!" Trey snaps.

"I shouldn't have encouraged this grave digging. I knew the truth and the outcome." I continue.

"Tell them!" Trey growls. I begin to cry.

"I'm... not Lync. I'm Lockie Saunders. I'm under witness protection." I cry.

Deccan quickly stands up and walks over to Callie. They both look distraught. Trey let go of me and walks back over to the grave and begins putting the mud back in.

"Prove it..." Callie says as a tear fell down her cheek.

"5 years ago my brother Killian killed my parents and attempted to kill me." I sniff.

"Dude..." Deccan interrupts.

"My birthday is 15th of the 9th 2008. And I have the scars that Killian left me." I continue.

I lift my hoodie and t-shirt to show my stab wound scars on my stomach. I then tip my head back to show the slash scar on my throat.

"Why did you lie to us all? Why did you pretend to be someone else?" Callie cries.

"I didn't lie; I'm not supposed to tell no one. I didn't pretend to be someone else... I was being me, I'm still me. I'm the complete opposite of Killian." I explain.

"You look like Killian..." Deccan says as he looks at his phone.

"People wouldn't know that without looking, man," I reply.

Callie glances over to Deccan's phone then looks back at me. Suddenly she grabs her phone and a smile appears on her face.

"Oh my god... how cute were you!" She giggles.

I walk over and look at her phone. It was a photo of me when I was 12 from a news article.

"You still have your cute freckles too!" She squeals.

"Ok calm down." I laugh.

"I think we should go to the library. Get more information about Killian... and you Lockie..." Deccan says with a smile.

"I can tell you more than the Internet dude. I saw everything unravel and lived through it." I explain.

"Well let's go back to the skate park and talk about it," Callie suggests.

"We better go now before the grave keeper sees this," Trey says as he walks over.

We exit the cemetery. Then we halt. There are 3 police cars and an unmarked car at the gates.

"We've been spotted and reported." Trey mutters.

"No shit Sherlock," Deccan mumbles.

My dad walks over with the police officers. The four officers have their handcuffs ready.

"Trey Foyer, Deccan Meadows, Callie Willis, and Lync McCarthy. We are arresting you on suspicion of breaking and entering, public vandalism, and grave robbery." My dad explains.

We all stand in shock as the police begin to put cuffs on us behind our backs.

"You do not need to say anything, but it may harm your defence if you do not mention when question something you later rely on in court. Anything you do says may be given in as evidence. Do you understand?" He continues.

None of us can speak we just nod. I feel like I am going to cry. I have disappointed my dad and messed up big time. I try to fight back the tears along with the lump in my throat.

Chapter 10

What Have I Done?

I sit at a desk with the handcuffs wrapped around the bar of the desk. I can feel the tears rolling down my cheeks, my leg bouncing up and down underneath. I tap my finger on the desk and look up at the clock.

"Lockie McCarthy?" A man asks as he enters the room.

"Yes?" I sniff.

"My name is Detective Carl Dunham. I will be interviewing you." He continues as he sits down across the desk.

Little do I know I am being recorded by the camera. Twitching out craving more drugs as I feel tired. I watch the Detective press the button on the recorder.

"Interview starting at 6.30 pm. My name is Detective Carl Dunham. Please state your name and date of birth for the interview." He asks as he places his file onto the desk.

"Lync McCarthy 15th of September 2008," I answer as I put my hands together on the desk.

"State your name before witness protection." He continues.

"Lockie Saunders," I add.

"OK. Want to tell me why you dug up your own grave?" He asks.

"I didn't. My friends did. I was just there." Says as I put my face down to my hands to rub my eyes.

"And you let them?" He continues.

"Well yeah... I didn't commit a crime." I reply as I sit up.

"Well you did Lync... you took part in breaking." He explains.

I sigh and put my head onto the desk in front of me. I hear the door open. I quickly look up and see it's my dad.

"Detective Kevin McCarthy enters the room at 6.35 pm." The Detective states for the recording.

"Why did you do it Lync?" My dad asks as he sits on the chair at the other side of the desk.

"I just went with the flow. I didn't do anything wrong." I splutter.

"You dug a grave in broad daylight." He states.

"My friends did! I didn't!" I yell. "Why would I dig my own grave?" I continue.

"Why was it done?" The Detective asks.

"Because of this stupid urban legend that the whole town doesn't believe is real!" I yell.

"Ending interview at 7.10 pm." The Detective states as he ended the recording.

The Detective grabs his stuff and walks out of the interview room. I sit in silence staring at the handcuffs around my wrists. I just want to go home.

"Why Lockie? How could you be so irresponsible?" My dad growls.

"It wasn't me!" I yell.

"From us taking you in at 12 years old, we were all stunned by how polite and well behaved you were. But this past week... I don't even know who you are anymore." My dad explains.

"Dad don't say that! I'm still me!" I cry.

"You're coming with me and going into a cell. This will be your punishment." He continues.

He un cuffs me from the desk and lead me to a cell. I felt ashamed and guilty. I can see how disappointed my dad is. He can never imagine me doing anything like this.

"Dad please don't put me in a cell! I'm sorry!" I beg as tears run down my cheeks.

"So am I." He says as we get to the cell.

He opens the cell door and I walk in. He removes the handcuffs and walks out closing the door behind him.

"Dad please don't do this! I'm sorry! Dad!" I scream as I hit the door.

I fall to the floor behind the door and begin to cry. I can't believe he has just left me here. I can't believe I'm in a cell-like criminal. All I can do is cry.

We arrive home. The entire car journey home is silent. I am still crying silent tears. Dad hasn't spoken to me since he got me out of the cell. I open the car door and slam it shut and head into the house.

"Lockie?" My mum says softly.

I turn to look at her. She can see instantly how upset I am.

"Your dad has done this many times with Piper. He doesn't love you any less." She explains.

"I'm going to bed." I sniff as I continue up the stairs.

My dad walks in as I go upstairs. I turn to face him he stands at the bottom of the stairs and watches me walk up.

"You didn't need to go that far with Lockie, Kevin. He's nothing like Piper." My mum says.

"It has taught him a valuable lesson and I have no sympathy for his tears." My dad grumbles.

I get into my bedroom and close the door. I grab my bag of drugs and key. I do the usual and take it from the key. I then throw myself onto my bed and scream into my pillow. I have never been the angry type. But it's all beginning to build on me. I begin punching my bed beneath me as I continue to scream.

"So this is why you have no ounce of anger in you..." Piper smirks whilst she was stood in the doorway.

"Get out!" I yell and throw a pillow at her.

"Wow, Lockie... what the hell has got into you?" She laughs.

"I said get out!" I growl.

"Fine... I was just checking on you." She continues as she walks out of my room.

I run over to the door and slam it shut. I kick it, punch it then throw my back onto it and slowly slouch to the floor. Where has this anger come from? This rage. I'm beginning to scare myself.

"Lockie! Get down here now!" My dad yells from the bottom of the stairs.

I get up from the floor and grab the door handle. I have second thoughts.

"Fuck you!" I scream as I boot the door with my whole foot.

Then I hear him march up the stairs. I step back and prepare myself. I can feel my blood boiling. Suddenly my dad throws my door open. His face is red and his eyes glaring at me.

"How dare you speak to me like that under my roof!" He booms as he walks towards me.

I glance to the door and see my mum and Piper standing there watching in shock.

"I've had enough of pretending I'm ok! I'm not ok! It takes you to arrest me to find that out!" I yell.

My dad grabs me by the neck of my t-shirt and pins me up against my wardrobe.

"Kevin stop!" My mum screams.

"Get off me! You're not my dad! You will never be my dad I hate you!" I yell.

Instantly my dad let's go of my t-shirt and I drop to the floor. I quickly stand up and walk out of my room pushing past my mum and Piper. Why did I just say that? I didn't mean it! What's happening to me?

I grab my bag in the hall and walk out of the front door. It's probably best I don't go back tonight.

I call Deccan as I walk the streets. I eagerly wait for him to answer his phone. I can't help but begin to get upset about what had happened back at home. It's not like me at all.

"Yo bro!" Deccan says. He sounds like he is in a great mood. Unlike myself.

"Hey man, what you up to?" I ask with a slight shake in my voice.

"At home after the event at the police station... you ok man? You don't sound great?" He asks.

"I've just got in a fight with my dad and walked out. Can I stay at yours tonight?" I ask as I continue walking the dark streets.

"Sure. Just drop me a text when you're here and I will meet you at the front. You know my street. House number 4289." Deccan explains.

"Thanks, man I appreciate it." I splutter.

"No worries bro. See you soon yeah?" Deccan reply.

"See you soon man," I say as I ended the call.

There was something that I didn't realize as I am walking the streets. I'm alone, it's dark... very dark. The worst part is that Killian is lurking around somewhere.

I quickly begin to pick up speed to get to Deccan's house. I put my hand in my pocket and grab my pack of cigarettes. As I continue walking I grab a cigarette out of the packet and grab my lighter from my other pocket. I light my cigarette, I look up and froze. A dark figure is standing a couple of feet away from me. It's still, so still, it making me feel uncomfortable.

"You dug my family's grave!" The figure growls as he points at me.

I begin to step back, step by step. My heart begins to race and the rush of adrenaline instantly made me feel sick to the stomach.

"I... I... I don't know what you're talking about..." I stutter.

"Don't play games with me kid!" He yells as he begins to creep towards me.

"Dude, I swear! You have the wrong person!" I snap as I quickly glance behind to find an escape route.

Suddenly the figure begins to laugh. It doesn't sound familiar to what Killian sounds like. I pause and squint my eyes at the figure in front of me.

"It's me you idiot!" He laughs as he pulls his hood down. It's Deccan.

"What the fuck man! That wasn't even funny." I snap as I walk towards him.

"Dude... I know the route you walk to mine and there is no way I'm letting you walk alone. Not with that crazy nut job running around." He explains followed with a smile.

"I appreciate it... just don't be a prick next time," I grumble as I brush past him.

Deccan chuckles then turns to follow me to his house. I know he is the jokester and prankster in our group but I never expected him to do it to me.

We get to Deccan's and head up to his bedroom. I know all of us haven't slept since the curse happened so I'm excited to find out his way of staying awake. We enter his bedroom and Deccan throws his keys onto his bed.

"So, this is my cave. What do you think?" He smirks as he does a girly twirl.

"It's liveable." I chuckle as I glance around his room.

"Come on! This is the dream. Full PC gaming set up to your left, PlayStation, Xbox set up here at the back..." He explains as he points it all out. "The best part! Wait for it." He continues as he ran past me to the side of his PC.

"Ta, da!" He says in excitement as he flings open the mini-fridge door.

"A fridge full of drinks that rot your insides... nice," I mumble followed with a slight smirk.

Deccan flops his arms and runs to his bedside drawers. He turns to me with a big smile on his face.

"I wasn't sure what you would like it so..." He says with suspense.

He opens his drawer and waves his hand to go over to him.

"You're becoming hard-core right? Got three types of drugs here. Each has different effects." He continues.

"I have my stuff on me..." I hint as I look into the drawer.

"Take a break... try some Lucy!" He laughs as he pulls out a small bag of pills.

I look at the bag then back at Deccan confused. I give him the look. The look to says 'what the hell are you talking about?' look.

"These keep you awake and give you the best high ever! But only take them in a safe place." He explains as he passes me the bag.

"Why not... let's do it then." I smile.

"Woo!" Deccan shouts.

He takes the bag from me and opens it. He brings a pill out and then I take one out. I look at him then look at the pill in between my finger and thumb.

"How long until it hits you?" I ask as I stare at the little dot pill.

"Between 20 minutes to 2 hours. Depends on the person." Deccan explains with a smile.

I nod. I stick my tongue out and place it on then look at Deccan.

"Yeah, let it dissolve on your tongue. You can put your tongue in your mouth though man..." He laughs.

I close my mouth and wait. I begin to feel nervous about how it may turn out. I have no idea about this drug and what it can do.

Chapter 11

I Think I'm Going To Die!

I and Deccan begin playing some sort of horror game on his PlayStation. I feel like nothing is happening since we took that drug. I still feel fine and nothing looks different.

"It's hereditary." Something whispers.

"What is?" I ask Deccan as I pause the game.

"What is what?" He asks me whilst looking at me confused.

"You say it was hereditary," I reply placing down control pad.

Deccan begins to look worried and places the control pad down next to the one I am using.

"Dude... I'm sorry I really shouldn't have given you that stuff. Come over to the bed." He asks as he offers me his hand.

I grab Deccan's hand and stand up. I turn to look in the mirror it wasn't me. I look like Killian.

"You can't escape it. You will soon fall." The voice whispers again.

"What the hell! What's happening?" I begin to scream.

"Lockie, chill!" Deccan shouts in my face as he grabs me by the sides of my arms.

"I don't look like me! I look like Killian!" I continue to yell.

Deccan pulls me to sit on the floor and he sits next to me. He grabs his phone from his pocket and begins to dial a number.

"Don't get him to come for me!" I cry as I try to grab the phone from him.

"Lockie! I'm not an enemy. I'm getting help." Deccan explains as he places the phone to his ear.

I try to grab the phone from him and begin to cry. I don't know what's going on or what's happening to me. One thing is for sure... I'm petrified.

"I'm not going to the psychiatric unit!" I scream.

Deccan looks at me in a way he has never looked at me before. He stands up and walks to the other side of his bedroom.

"Yo dude. You need to get down to mine ASAP. I messed up..." Deccan says to the person on the phone.

"Yeah, I'll text her now." He continues.

He hangs up and quickly types on his phone. He then throws his phone onto the bed and he walks over to me and sits down.

"Don't take this the wrong way but... hold my hands." He says as he holds his hands out to me. I nod and grab them.

"Breathe with me." He says as he takes a deep breath.

"It's been a long time coming." A voice whispers again.

"Get out my head!" I scream. I let go of Deccan's hands and put my hands over my ears and place my head down on my legs.

"It will get better." The voice whispers.

"You will become you." The whispering continues.

"Deccan! Help me!" I cry.

Deccan sits next to me and begins to rub my back with his hand.

"I'm sorry man. You need to ride it out, Trey and Callie are on their way to help." He explains.

I start to feel like I can't breathe like something is crushing my chest. My heart starts racing; I feel like I could have a heart attack. I can't help but cry. I feel like I'm going insane but at the same time, I feel like I'm going to die.

"Deccan! I think I'm going to die!" I cry.

"Calm down dude you're safe. Try and relax." He reassures with a smile.

How can I relax? I can't control all that is happening to me. What if I hurt someone? What if I do have undiagnosed Imply-Psychosis? All these thoughts and questions I keep asking whilst I feel I am turning into Killian. I'm scared.

Trey and Callie walk through the door. Callie runs over to me and Deccan and Trey close the door.

"How could you be so stupid?" Callie yells at Deccan as she puts her arms around me.

"I'm sorry I didn't think." He says as he moves away from my side.

I move my hands from my ears and wrap them around my legs and begin to rock back and forth.

"It's a good job my parents are away..." Deccan mumbles as he approaches his bed and sits down.

"Is this the only stuff he's had?" Trey asks as he stands next to me.

"I don't know... I think so." Deccan shrugs.

I pause and shake my head. I continue to rock back and forth

"Is he able to speak?" Callie asks.

"He hasn't spoke since before you got here," Deccan explains as he folds his arms.

Trey walks over to Deccan and smacks him at the back of the head.

"Ouch!" He yells as he rubs his head. Trey shrugs.

"Lync? Have you had anything else?" Callie asks softly into my ear.

I stop rocking and nod. I lift my head from my knees to see everyone looking at each other in panic. I gently push Callie away from me and stand up. I stand in front of Deccan's mirror and stare.

"Lync? Are you ok?" Trey asks as he slowly walks over to me.

I feel the tears rolling down my cheeks. The reflection isn't me and it isn't changing. It's Killian. Black hair, white skin... my clothes are the same style that he wore. I feel like I'm turning into him. Becoming what he is.

"Why are you calling me that?" I ask as I continue to stare at the mirror.

"If you prefer Lockie that's fine too," Callie adds as she walks over and places her hand on my shoulder.

I feel anger. It wasn't just any anger I've felt before. I feel so angry I need a release. I clench my fists and begin to shake. I feel my body burning up as if my blood is at boiling point.

"Lockie are you ok?" Callie asks as she looks at me then back at the mirror.

"Get off me!" I growl and push her hand off me.

Before I can think about my actions I let out a scream of anger and punch the mirror with full force. It instantly smashes as I hit it. I pull my fist away and open my hand out. Small shards of the mirror is stuck into my knuckles. Deep gashes where I had hit the mirror. But... the anger was still there. I turn to everyone as I look at my hand then look up to them. Trey, Callie, and Deccan all stood in shock and fear.

"This isn't like him. He's always been too nice to be like this." Callie whispers to Trey and Deccan.

"Lockie? Breathe. You're beginning to scare us." Trey says calmly.

I quickly walk towards them and push past to the door. I pull the door open and run downstairs. I hear everyone follow behind.

I get onto the streets kicking and punching everything I walk past. I head towards the skate park. As I get to the gates Trey grab the back of my hoodie. I stop.

"I know you might lash out at me, but we are here for you. No matter what." Trey explains then let's go.

I continue to the gates and get onto the park. The anger, the rage builds again but worse. I need to try and gain control.

I wake up on the grass next to the skate park. I look at my hands; they're covered in blood. I try to move my fingers but the pain was too much. My head hurt so much that I vomit next to myself.

"Can we approach you now?" Deccan asks.

I look up, it was still dark. Deccan, Trey, and Callie are stood in front of me.

"I don't remember getting here... what happened?" I ask as I rub my head.

"To put it bluntly you turned into a psychopath. And I do mean you were on the same level as your brother," Trey explains as he folds his arms.

"No... I've never had that type of anger before. I don't even think that type of anger exists with me." I splutter as I slowly stand up.

"You surprised us all Lockie. You do have that anger within you and it scared us all." Callie adds.

"Call someone to take us to hospital. Please." I ask as I try to hold back the vomiting again.

Trey huffs and dials on his phone. He walks away from us as he waits to speak to the person.

"So I had a rage frenzy... whilst high..." I say quietly.

"That's what it looked like." Deccan interrupts.

"So I could become a monster?" I cry as I fall back to the floor.

Callie runs over to me and kneels next to me. I look up at her and she smiles.

"We will get through it. You're not a monster and you have more chance than Killian had to get better." She explains as she strokes my face.

I begin to cry but I smile back. Trey runs back over to us and puts his phone back in his pocket.

"A good friend is on her way. She doesn't live far so let's get him up and help him to the entrance." Trey explains as he walks over to me.

Deccan nods and walks over to the other side of me. They both lift my arms and put them around their shoulders.

"Come on then let go." Deccan smiles as he begins to walk.

Callie follows behind as Trey and Deccan carry me.

We stand on the path by the road. Deccan and Trey still holding me up. A dark colour land rover pulls up in front of us. The window winds down.

"Miss Jenkins?" I ask whilst squinting through the window.

"No time for talking just yet. Get in!" She says as she turns off the ignition.

Trey and Deccan help me climb into the back. Deccan gets in first and helps me in and Trey climbs in next to me. Callie jumps in the front seat. Trey shuts the door behind us.

"Go, go, go!" Trey yells.

Miss Jenkins turns on the ignition and drives off down the road.

Everyone sits quietly as Miss Jenkins drives to the hospital. I'm becoming confused as to why Trey called her.

"So why did you call Miss Jenkins?" I ask Trey.

"Because she knows what to do." He replies bluntly.

"Out of school, you don't need to call me Miss Jenkins." She giggles as she glances at me through the rear view mirror.

"What do I call you then?" I ask with a smile.

"Penny. My name is Penny." She answers.

"Your brother's ex," Deccan whispers to me.

I sit in shock. I didn't know about Killian and Penny being together. I can't believe it's Penny! She looks different now.

I've got bad memories of this hospital. Firstly, when I had to get rushed in after Killian tried killing me. Secondly when Callie was close to being killed because of the curse.

Wait... the curse is probably the cause of me being the way I was. But the next question is... why is it not affecting Trey and Deccan anymore?

"You're going to be ok Lockie," Callie reassures as she grabs my hand.

I nod. We walk into the hospital, Penny went to the reception desk as everyone lead me to the waiting area.

"Trey? Deccan?" I say, they both turned to look at me.

"Why does it feel like I'm slowly going insane and acting like a psychopath when you two seem normal?" I ask as I stare at them.

Callie looks at me then glares at Trey and Deccan. They both look down at the floor in shame.

"We... got rid of it..." Trey mumbles as he twiddles his thumbs.

"You did what?" I yell as I quickly stand up. The entire waiting room stare but I don't care at this point.

"What kind of friends are you? You've done that behind my back and left me to suffer the consequences knowing damn well about my background!" I continue to yell.

I feel the anger building again and my body burning up. I had to get out of the waiting area. Quickly.

"You know what? Fuck you." I growl as I storm off towards the toilet.

"Lockie! Wait!" Callie shouts as she follows behind.

I open the toilet door and quickly shut it behind me. I lock it and put my back to the door. My breathing becomes faster, my heart racing. I place my hand on my face and begin to cry.

"Lockie? Open the door." Callie asks softly from behind the door.

"No! Stay away from me. I'm turning into a monster. I don't want to hurt you." I cry and slid down the door to the floor.

"Lockie, it's Penny. Open the door." She asks.

I begin to shake. The more I think about what Trey and Deccan did the more the rage boils.

"I can't!" I yell as I stand up.

I begin to hear whispering that didn't sound clear. Starting quietly and beginning to get louder and louder. I grab the back of my hair and my arms over my face. I start to growl in anger.

"Get out of my head!" I scream then start to hit my head with my fists.

"Open the door now! We need you out of there!" Callie cries.

Suddenly the whispering stops and I collapse.

Chapter 12

I'm Not Him

I awake in a hospital bed. I look at my arm and see that I am attached to a drip. I turn to look to my right and see my mum, dad and Piper sitting there.

"I'm sorry," I whisper.

"You don't need to be. You're safe and that's all we care about now." My mum replies with a smile.

I look at my dad who is sat with his arms folded looking at me as if he still holds a grudge against me from the other night.

"Dad, that wasn't me," I say as tears begin to build up in my eyes.

"I know son, we all know. We're all here to help you through this." He says with a smile as he unfolds his arms.

Suddenly the door opens. There is no surprise to who walks in.

"Lockie Saunders." The doctor says with a creepy smile.

"Hello, again doctor creep," I grumble as I stare him down.

He looks at my family and nods. My dad nods back and they all stand up and begin to walk to the door.

"Wait! You can't go!" I yell. My throat burns as I yell. It felt as if I have drank freshly boiled water.

"You need to rest son. The doctor here is the best in the psychiatric unit, he will help you." My dad explains as he opens the door.

"But he's a psycho himself! You almost arrested him!" I continue.

"We got the doctor's story and it seemed like you had this condition all along. He explained it to us so we couldn't arrest him for trying to help you." My dad explains with a smile.

"No! He's lying! Don't leave me!" I scream.

"We'll see you shortly darling. Love you." My mum says as she closes the door.

I can't help but stare at the door. Tears streaming down my cheeks. I slowly turn to look at the doctor who gives off an eerie smile as he pushes his glasses up his nose with his finger.

"So, you manipulated everyone against Killian?" I croak.

"No. It's not manipulation, it's truth." He smirks as he looks down at the file and flicks through it.

I look at my cannula and the bandages around my hands. Then I look to the door and back at doctor creep who is still scanning through the file.

"This is going to hurt like hell but screws it," I say to myself.

I rip the cannula out and quickly jump from the bed. I run towards the door.

"I wouldn't do that if I was you, Lockie." The doctor says.

I turn around to look at him. I can feel the blood trickling down my arm from where the cannula was. He smiles at me. I open the door and two big guys are stood staring at me.

"Oh, Lockie. You're definitely like your brother, he never listened either." The doctor sighs and places the notes down on the table.

"I want to go home," I say quietly. It is all I can do as I'm starting to lose my voice.

"You can't go home. And if you try to go home you will get sectioned which means you need to live here." He continues.

"I'm not him. I'm not Killian." I reply.

The doctor nods and grabs his notes. He walks towards me near the door.

"You're right but you have the second strain so you'll be worse." He chuckles as he leaves.

I can't help but stand in shock. I glance over to my bed and run over I grab my rucksack from the side. I quickly open it and rummage through to check I have everything. I zip it shut and throw it over my shoulder. I walk over to the door and open it slightly to check if the guards have gone. They aren't there which gives me an opportunity. I walk out of my room closing the door behind me as I scan the corridors up and down. I turn left to follow the way out signs. I grab my phone from the side pocket of my bag and call Trey.

"I'm not your friend before you ask. I need you to send me Penny's number now!" I demand as I rush through the corridors.

"Ok, but why?" He asks.

"Just send it to me goddammit! I can't talk!" My voice cracks as I attempt to yell.

I look up and see the doctor walking towards me with his 2 guards. I turn right into the toilet shutting the door quickly.

"Shit!" I whisper to myself as I grab my bag from my shoulder.

I open my bag and grab my hoodie. I rush to get it on. I zip my bag up and zip my hoodie up. I throw the rucksack onto my shoulder and put my hood up. Slowly I open the door. I take a glance I can't see him or his guards. I walk out holding my head low towards the exit. Suddenly my phone rings. Trey has sent me Penny's number. Quickly I press call. I head towards the road from the hospital premises.

"Hello?" Penny answer.

"Penny! It's Lockie please help me." I cry.

"Lockie! What's going on?" She asks worryingly.

"I've escaped out of the hospital. That doctor is a psycho he wants to section me! I've done nothing to be sectioned." I continue as my voice squeaks.

"Ok calm down. Meet me at the shops, they're 10 minutes away from the hospital." She explains.

"Sure," I whisper.

Penny hangs up and I power walk to the shops whilst keeping an eye out for the doctor. Surely he won't look for me out here.

I stand outside the shops waiting. The weather isn't nice like usual, it is gloomy and heavily raining. People are walking past me looking at me, staring. I feel ill, I'm cold and dripping wet. I look at the floor and put my bandaged hands in my pockets. Suddenly I hear a car pull up and beep. I look up and it was Penny's land rover. I walk over and quickly open the door. I jump in and slam it shut. I sit silently with my head down.

"Lockie, what have you done?" She asks softly.

I shrug and stay silent.

"I could get in a lot of trouble if I get caught with you. You do know that?" She says as she leans over to try and look at me.

"The doctor... he will... make me... worse..." I splutter.

"Which doctor?" Penny asks.

"The one... who treated... Killian..." I whisper.

"Oh god. Not him!" She blurts out.

I nod. I hear her sit back in her seat. I look up at her and she turns to look at me.

"Please... help me." I sniff.

Penny softly pulls my hood down and places her hand on my cheek.

"I promise I will." She whispers with a smile.

She turns the heating off and drives off onto the road.

We arrive at Penny's house. She throws her keys onto the couch, I follow behind her.

"Kylie! You can go now sweet!" She shouts.

A girl not much younger than me walks into the living room. Brown short hair, well-done makeup, and a beautiful smile. Until she looks at me. Her smile drops.

"Anytime..." She says as she looks at me up and down.

"Who's he?" She asks as she looks at Penny.

"An old friend of mine, Lync." Penny says with a smile.

Kylie nods and walks past me. She gets into the hall and grabs her coat.

"Message me if you need me Pen." She says as she leaves.

I look around and notice kid's toys in the corner of the living room. I look back at Penny. Suddenly a little girl runs into the living from.

"Mummy!" She screams with happiness as she hugs Penny.

"You're a mum?" I ask.

"Who's that mummy?" The little girl asks as she looks at me.

Penny smiles at me and then smiles at the little girl.

"April, this is your uncle Lockie. He's your daddy's brother." She smiles.

What! Killian has a... daughter? What?

"W-what?" I stutter.

April runs over to me and wraps her arms around me. I look down at her then back to Penny.

"I kept her. I lied to everyone saying I was having an abortion but I couldn't go through with it." Penny explains as she looks at us in awe.

"So my brother... is a... dad?" I splutter.

Penny nods and smiles again.

"April? Go upstairs and play with your dolls. I'll shout you when your dinner is ready." She says sweetly.

"Ok mummy!" April reply as she let go of me and ran upstairs.

"So first things first. You need to look different so you don't get caught." Penny points out.

"What do you mean?" I croak.

Penny put her finger up and runs through the door and upstairs. I look around and try to get my head around the fact that Killian is a dad. Suddenly Penny runs back into the living room.

"Hair dye and hair cut?" She says with a giggle.

"No! I like my hair the way it is! I have to have it straight, if it's shorter than this it's horrible and wavy!" I attempt to yell.

"It's either that or you get caught, Lockie." Penny sighs.

"Fine..." I huff.

Penny walks into the kitchen and I follow her. She pulls a chair out from the table.

"Sit down. I'll do your hair cut first." She says as she begins to prepare the scissors and combs.

The thought of my hair being brown begins to make my stomach turn. If people say I look like Killian now I sure will with brown hair.

"Ready?" Penny smiles.

"Just do it," I mumble as I close my eyes.

Two hours later and it's done. I haven't seen what I look like yet. I don't want to.

"Close your eyes! I'll guide you to the mirror," Penny says with excitement.

I close my eyes and Penny begins to steer me to the living room. She turns me then stops.

"Open!" She says with a grin.

I open my eyes. I don't even recognize myself... my hair is still slightly long but I've always straightened it. It's weird seeing it wavy. I've never dyed my hair... so being a brunette made me look more ill than I already did.

"I look so ill..." I grumble.

"Once you get your colour back you'll suit it. You look different!" She giggles.

"I look like my brother," I mumble as I turn away from the mirror.

"Lockie, you look fine." She smiles.

Penny then heads into the kitchen to start dinner. She has already put my hoodie and clothes into the drier. I go into the hall to get my phone from my rucksack. I look and see I have 100 missed calls. My heart stops. I unlock my phone and scroll through. Mum, dad, Piper, unknown. I dial Callie's number and wait for her to answer.

"Lockie!" She shouts.

"I need to meet you," I say quietly.

"You do realize the police and your family are looking for you?" She says.

"Trust me I know. But meet me near Dead Man's Woods entrance." I explain.

"They will find you, Lockie. They know what you look like." She says sternly.

I look in the hall mirror. In front of me.

"Trust me they won't," I reply.

"If you're sure. Meet me there in 10!" She says.

"Not a problem," I reply as I hang up.

I put my phone in my pocket and make my way to the kitchen where Penny is.

"Silly question... have you got any piercings for lip and ear?" I ask.

Penny turns to look at me.

"Funnily yes. I bought some back when I wanted them and never wore them. I'll grab them for you." She smiles as she brushes past me.

It didn't take her long to come back downstairs. She opens her hand there are 2 lip bars and fake stretcher piercing.

"I trust you to pierce my lip and ear... don't fuck up!" I say with a slight smile.

Penny nods and goes to her cupboard in the kitchen where She grabs a needle. She runs over to her freezer and grab some ice.

"OK, are you ready?" She asks as she shows me.

I nod and close my eyes. She places the ice on my bottom lip until it is so cold and becomes numb. She quickly put the needle through and swaps it for the lip bar. She continues to do the same on the other side. Last one is my ear. She holds the ice to my ear as she did with my lip. Then she puts the needle through then puts the stretcher piercing in.

"Done!" She says as she walks back into the kitchen.

I turn to look in the mirror. I love it! I look different now so hopefully, I won't be recognized. I walk into the kitchen and go to the dryer. I grab my clothes.

"So you're braving going out now?" Penny asks as she stirs dinner in the pan.

"Yeah. I won't be out long." I reply with a slight smile.

"Be careful." She says worryingly.

I nod and head into the living room to get changed.

I get dressed and throw my hood up. I grab my phone and put it in my pocket. I put both hands in my pockets to cover the bandages.

"See you later!" I shout to Penny.

"See you later. Text me if you need picking up!" She shouts back.

I open the front door and quietly close it behind me. And head down the drive to the street.

Chapter 13

It's My Fate

Dead Man's Woods is famous now because of Killian. I stand and wait for Callie. I begin to dither, I put my bandaged hands in my pockets. Thankfully it's not raining so I'm happy to stand here. Suddenly I see Callie but she's not alone. She's with Trey and Deccan. I wave to them, they clock me and walk towards me.

"What are you playing at!" Callie screams as she pushes me. I hold my hands up.

"What do you mean?" I ask quietly.

Trey storms over to me and pulls my hood down. They all look at me in disbelief.

"Holy Lord," Deccan mumbles.

"It's me, Lockie," I whisper.

"You don't even look like you..." Trey points out.

"He sounds like him..." Deccan interrupts.

"Your parents are calling us every 10 minutes!" Callie continues.

Then Trey's phone begins to ring. He looks at me and pulls his phone out of his pocket then looks at his phone.

"Tell me about it..." He grumbles as he shows me that it is my dad calling.

"Don't answer it!" I hiss.

Trey sighs and answers the call. He puts it on the loudspeaker.

"Trey! Please tell me you've seen him?" My dad panics.

I wave my hands and shake my head.

"No. We've checked everywhere we hang out," Trey replies bluntly.

"We just want him home!" My mum screams in the background.

"If you hear from him tell us. Thea is distraught here!" My dad explains.

It hurt like hell hearing my mum screaming and crying in the background. It's hard hearing my dad panicking and worrying about me.

"Sure Mr. McCarthy I'll call if I find him." Trey murmurs.

"Thanks, Trey." My dad replies then hangs up.

Everyone looks at me after that call. I feel guilty. I've run away from the hospital and home. It's killing them not finding me.

"If the sound of your parents heartbroken doesn't get you to go home, I don't know what will," Callie mumbles as she walks off.

Trey and Deccan look at me up and down and shake their heads. They turn to follow Callie.

"It's not them!" I manage to shout.

They stop and turn to look at me.

"It's the psychiatric doctor. He made Kil worse and used him as a guinea pig to gain information on Imply-Psychosis. He wanted to do the same with me." I explain.

I begin to cry at the thought of it.

"He's manipulated my parents to make them think he will make me better. But he won't. He will make me worse!" I cry.

"I don't have Imply-Psychosis, I had drugs in my system that cause me to become aggressive. I'm sorry everyone..." I say followed by a sigh.

Callie walks over to me and smiles. She grabs my hand softly.

"We will help you. But first, we need to make sure your parents know you're safe." She explains with a smile.

I look over to Trey and Deccan they stand and watch. Then again, I wouldn't be the way I am if I don't have the curse and the stupid drugs inside me.

I get to my house. I open the front gate and pause. I feel sick as I know what is going to happen next. I turn to look at Trey, Deccan and Callie they nod at me. I slowly turn back to face my house and take a deep breath. I walk up the path to the door and open it. I quietly sneak in hoping that they won't hear me. The living room door opens.

"Lockie! You've come home!" Piper cries as she wraps her arms around me.

"Err, yeah I have," I mumble.

My mum and dad quickly rush to the door and look at me in shock.

"What have you done to your hair and face?" My mum asks disappointingly.

"I didn't want to get caught." I sniff as I gently push Piper from me.

"What you did was stupid Lockie. You will get sectioned when you go back now!" My dad snaps.

"I'm not going back. I don't have Imply-Psychosis." I reply bluntly.

I begin to head upstairs. The more I thought about how my hair looks the more I want to get it back right.

"You've shown symptoms of it, Lockie. We've seen it for ourselves." My mum explains.

I stop halfway up the stairs and turn to face my family who are gathered at the bottom.

"Truth is... I did the psycho dare and got the curse. That turned from bad to worse so I begin taking different drugs to keep me awake which made the curse worse. I don't have Imply-Psychosis. If I did or do, I will admit myself to hospital." I explain then turn to continue up the stairs.

I got into my bedroom and grab some clothes out of my drawers. I think about the next steps before I get taken to the hospital again. It will be best if I get rid of this curse for a start.

I grab my travel bag and throw everything I need into it. I grab my straighteners from the side of my wardrobe and put them into my bag. I pause. I look around my bedroom. I can't leave my family worrying again as I have, maybe it would be best if I stayed. I leave my bag on the bed and head back downstairs.

I walk into the living room and see everyone sit there looking upset. They just want to protect me. That's what they've done for the past 5 years.

"I'll stay." I splutter.

They all look up at me. My mum slowly stands up and walks over and hugs me.

"We just want you to be safe darling. We love you." She whispers into my ear.

"I know. The anger isn't me; you know me well enough to know something was causing it." I whisper back.

My mum let go of me and places her hands onto my cheeks and smiles.

"I know darling. We will protect you, I promise." She says quietly.

I nod and pull away from her slowly as I look at my dad and Piper sit on the couch.

"You've got to trust me. I'm nothing like Kil and if I know that I'm going in that direction I will admit it." I explain.

My dad smiles and nods and I nod back. I turn to smile at my mum then walk out of the living room to the front door.

"I will be back later. I need to sort this mess out." I shout to them as I open the front door.

I head out of the door and see that Trey, Deccan, and Callie are still waiting. I head over to them to arrange a plan.

"Right guys, first I need this curse removing. I need to get my hair back to normal so I need to get the stuff from the market." I explain with a smile.

Callie smiles, Trey and Deccan nod. I walk towards them and then lead the way to Trey's house. Hopefully, everything goes to plan without falling like I already have.

Trey opens his front door. As we follow behind him Quin is standing in the kitchen doorway across from us.

"What's happening guys?" Quin asks as he folds his arms.

"We messed up dad. It wasn't just me and Deccan with the curse, it was Lockie too." Trey explains and holds his head in shame.

Quin's facial expression instantly drops. He unfolds his arms and walks over to Trey. Suddenly he grabs him by his t-shirt and pulls him to his face.

"Are you stupid? How could you be so careless!" He yells in Trey's face.

"I'm sorry!" Trey yells as fear begins to build in his face.

"It's not safe for Lockie to get this! I didn't think you could be so irresponsible!" Quin continues.

"Can we just remove it before I have another anger outburst?" I butt in.

Quin looks at me whilst still gripping Trey's t-shirt tightly. He then let go and Trey instantly drops to the floor.

"You've... had an... anger outburst?" He stutters whilst giving me a worried look.

"Yeah..." I say whilst looking at Trey and Deccan.

"Ok... we will remove the curse but monitor these outbursts," Quin explains as he walks into the side room.

Trey stands up and shrugs then follows Quin into the room. I turn to look at Deccan and Callie they smile and follow Trey, I take a deep breath and follow behind.

I sit feeling anxious and scared. I don't know what to expect this time around. Trey walks over to me and smiles. He holds a blindfold up to show me then steps towards me to place it on.

"Tie his hands to the chair," Quin demands.

"What?" I shout.

Before I can move both my arms were tied to the chair at the same time. Now I'm feeling like I'm not safe.

"Don't panic Lockie, I'm going to remove the curse and a little extra besides," Quin explains calmly.

I sit and wait. I begin to hear whispering again, the creepy whispering. Quin places his hand on my head.

"3, 2, 1..." Quin clicks his fingers.

I open my eyes and notice I no longer have the blindfold on, I wasn't tied to the chair either. I look to my right and see everyone stand there smiling.

"How are you feeling?" Quin asks as he crosses his leg another the other.

"I feel fine why?" I ask. I feel confused as to why I was sat here.

"What can you tell us about Killian?" Callie asks as she walks over to me.

"Who's that?" I question as I rub my head.

Everyone looks at each other and high five each other.

"What's your name?" Deccan asks as he walks beside Callie.

"Lync McCarthy... Why is everyone quizzing me? My head is beginning to hurt." I ask as I stand from the chair.

Everyone looks at one another silently. I walk to the door and look into the mirror as I pass. I still look the same... Blonde hair, straight... just... it's a bit shorter than I remember.

"Who's cut my hair?" I ask as I stare into the mirror.

I still hear everyone whispering. I turn around to see what they are doing.

"I did it by accident remember? I gave you trim but took too much off." Callie explains.

I shrug and open the door. I head out to the front yard trying to figure out what the hell was going on. I feel something is off. I need to know what. The more I try to think about it the more frustrated I become. I feel something has been blocked. I pull my hood up and run down the street towards my parent's house.

Chapter 14

I'm Not An Angry Person

I need to search inside this bedroom high and low. I need answers! Nothing is making sense. I run over to my desk draw and start looking for something that I will remember.

"Lockie, is that you, sweetie?" My mum shouts to me.

I stop digging through my drawer. Something clicks. I quickly shut my desk drawer and head downstairs.

"Mum!" I shout to see where she goes.

"Kitchen!" She shouts back.

I open the kitchen door and she is seated at the table on her laptop with a coffee.

"My name!" I shout as I begin gasping for breath from running.

"Lockie... why?" She replies with a confused look.

"Saunders? Like Killian Saunders?" I ask as I pull the chair out from under the table.

"Yes... he's your brother... are you taking again?" She asks worryingly.

"Taking? Drugs, no! I can't remember!" I yell as I throw myself into the chair.

My mum slowly closes her laptop and stares at me. She gently removes her glasses and places them on top of her laptop.

"Have you been to Quin's by any chance?" She asks with a smirk.

"Yes... why?" I ask as I lean over the table.

"He's wiped your recent memories for some reason." She replies.

It all starts to fall into place. My name is Lync McCarthy under witness protection. Killian is my brother. I take drugs for something but I don't think that's relevant. And I have that curse... that's what Quin removed with some memories.

"Better luck to him next time the prick," I grumble as I push myself from the table.

I head to the back door then turn to my mum who places her glasses back onto her nose.

"I'll be back later," I reassure before opening the door.

She turns to me and nods. Hopefully, I will get some answers from everyone on why they did this. I will never forget these memories anymore, ever.

I arrive back at Trey's house. I'm feeling quite angry since they went and did this without my consent. I knock on the door then step back. It didn't take long for Trey to answer.

"You're back! Where did you go?" He asks as he leans onto the door frame.

"Get out my way." I hiss and push past him.

I get into the hallway and see Deccan and Callie on the stairs. Quin steps into the hallway from the kitchen wiping his hands on a towel.

"So who is the one that thought it was a brave idea to take my memories again?" I growl as I storm into the hallway.

Callie looks down at the steps before her. Deccan and Trey look at her then look at Quin. I begin to get the idea that it was Callie's idea.

"Please don't tell me it was you, Callie?" I snap as I step in her direction.

"I'm sorry Lockie. I wanted to help you, I want the old you back." She answers as tears begin to fill her eyes.

"Why do you want the 'old me' back so badly?" I yell.

"Because I have feelings for you! I have from the beginning before all this shit!" She announces as the tears rolls down her cheeks.

I instantly shut up, everyone is silent. I look at Trey, Deccan, and Quin, they knew about her feelings. I can tell by the look on their faces.

"Why did you not tell me?" I ask calmly.

"Because... I'm a girly girl, I didn't think I was your type..." She cries.

I'm in shock. How can everyone keep this from me? Yes, I've seen her as a friend and she has given me hints without me realizing until now. She cares too much about me, she's held my hand at my worst and she's been there through the tears.

"You could have told me. We could have at least tried to hit it off with dates and stuff." I explain.

"What do mean by could?" Deccan interrupts.

"I'm not in the right place man. Look what happened with Kil and Penny, I don't want Callie to go through that." I continue as I walk over to the door.

"I want to be there for you Lockie! I want to help and guide you through it all." Callie admits as she began to walk towards me.

I turn to her and place my bandaged hand upon her cheek. I smile then gently kiss her on her other cheek.

"I know you still will be there for me. Just wait for me yeah? Maybe when this is over and if I'm still sane we can try." I whisper into her ear.

I pull away from her and notice a smile appear on her face. I turn to everyone else and nod before walking out of the door.

I arrive back home and notice my dad is home early from work. I think it would be wise to have the tests done for Imply-Psychosis to be safe. Just not at that hospital.

"Dad?" I shout as I open the front door.

He appears at the top of the stairs and I jump in fright.

"Sorry son did I scare you?" He asks.

"No... anyway, can I go to the mental health facility at Lakeside hospital?" I ask with a smile.

"Err... sure. What is it for son?" He questions as he begin to walk downstairs.

"Just want to make sure I'm completely sane." I chuckle.

He nods and grabs his coat from the hook. He turns to grab his keys from the key hook behind the door.

"Well, we will need to go now as I and your mum have plans tonight." He explains

"Sure." I smile back as I walk to the car.

The lakeside hospital is in the opposite direction as Wilfred Hospital. Wilfred is the one with the institute attached to it where Killian lived. The one that doctor creep works at. I'm hoping I get my results today for these tests.

"I'm nervous," I mumble as I stand and stare at the hospital ahead.

"If you have it, it's better to know now." My dad reassures me.

I take a deep breath and walk towards the entrance. I walk into the building first and sit down. My dad tells reception everything to try and push me in quicker for the tests. It didn't take long until he came over to sit with me.

"Shouldn't take time son." My dad whispers.

We've been waiting for thirty minutes in the waiting area. I begin to get irritated. The thought of being here was beginning to get to me.

"Lync McCarthy?" The doctor shouts.

I take a deep breath and walk over to meet him. My dad follows.

"Hi Lync, take it you have come for some tests done for your mental health?" He asks with a smile.

"Yeah, I want to find out if I have the same condition as my brother," I explain.

He nods and opens the side room door.

"Have a seat in there for me." He says as he holds his hand out to the room.

I step in and he closes the door behind me. Then I hear a click. I look in front of me where there was a large mirror. I look around the room and see a small coffee table with seats around. But what I don't understand is why I have been locked in.

"Ok... you can come in and tell me what's happening now..." I shout out into the room.

"Lockie, can you hear me?" The doctor says through a speaker.

"Yeah... Why am I here? Why are you calling me Lockie now?" I ask as I begin to feel panicky.

"This is the test room. We use multiple things to trigger any reactions that indicate Imply-Psychosis." He explains.

I take a deep breath and close my eyes. Composure at its finest.

"What if I tell you that I am sending in 2 guards to get you prepared for our mental health facility?" The doctor proposes.

"Depends if it's true?" I ask as I look towards the door.

Suddenly the door unlocks and the two guys from Wilfred Hospital enter the room. Instantly I go from 0 to 100. I begin to back away as I felt my body burning up, I began to feel sick and a headache starting to fire up.

"Get away from me!" I growl as I step back to the wall.

"The guards aren't going to touch you, Lockie. Not unless I tell them to." The doctor explains.

My heart was pounding; my body began to shake in anger.

"Now." The doctor says.

Suddenly the goons come over to me and pin my arms and legs to the floor. I begin to scream as loud as I can for them to get off me. Before I know it the doctor walks in with a blood pressure machine, heart monitor, and needle. He begins to wire me up.

"Get off me!" I scream as I continue to try and kick out.

I feel the tears rolling down my cheeks. The guard with my arms looks at me then shakes his head. He looks at the doctor who is noting all my results down. He finishes then looks at me. He doesn't look happy about the results. He stands up and leaves, the guards do the same. Just as they shut the door I jump up to try and open it. They have locked it again. I kick it then punch it but nothing is working. I turn around to the table and chairs and begin to flip them over and kick them across the room whilst still screaming until my throat went numb. Suddenly I pass out.

I awake in a hospital bed with my dad by my side. He grabs my hand and smiles.

"What happened?" I ask.

"You had a test done and had another outburst. You didn't cry tears either... it was blood. Then you collapsed and blacked out after it." My dad explains.

I can't help but begin to get upset. I didn't realize how bad it is. The doctor walks in with my file and sits next to my bed. He opens my file and flicks through to my results.

"So it does appear you have Imply-Psychosis and you've entered phase 3 of it." He explains with a disappointing look.

"So is that bad?" I ask.

"Yes, it is. We can try you on medications but I'm afraid you're past the point of controlling it." He replies.

No... this can't be happening! I can't have it! I'm not like Killian. What's going on...

"I can't have it! I can't turn out like him!" I cry as I grab my dad's hand.

"We will make sure that won't happen, son. I promise!" My dad says.

"I'll leave you alone to make the decision Mr. McCarthy." The doctor says as he gives my dad a nod and he leaves the room.

"Call mum and Piper!" I yell as I cling to his arm.

My dad grabs his phone from his pocket with his other hand and begin to dial my mum's number.

"Thea, can you come to Lakeside Hospital? It's about Lockie." He asks.

"Yeah, he has a diagnosis..." My dad pauses and looks at me sadly.

"He has it, same as Killian did." He continues.

He hangs up and places his phone back into his pocket. He turns to look at me, I can see the tears in his eyes. The hurt. The pain.

"You haven't failed me," I say with a smile as I slowly let go of his arm.

"We have. We should have done all this sooner. We should have taken precautions and dealt with it." He replies as he begins to cry.

"You're the best dad I've ever had. You're doing great, you haven't failed me. So please, stop thinking that." I continue whilst pushing myself up in the bed.

My dad gives a slight smile and grabs me for a hug. I can feel him hugging me tighter and tighter.

"I promise you now, you won't turn into the monster Killian is. I'll do everything in my power to prevent that." He whispers into my ear.

"I know you will dad, I know you will," I whisper back as I lay my head onto his shoulder.

The door opens, my mum and Piper walk into the room. My mum instantly drops her handbag and runs over to me. My dad pulls away from me to allow my mum to hug me. She wraps her arms around me and hugs me similar to my dad's. She let go and holds me by my arms and looks at me.

"Please make the right decision," I say quietly.

My mum turns to look at my dad. He nods and stands up and heads out of the room.

My mum begins to pack my stuff from the side table into my rucksack.

"I'm coming home?" I ask as I watch her pack my bag.

"Yes darling like we say to you, we won't let you turn out like Killian." She says with a beaming smile.

I throw the hospital sheets off me and quickly climb out of the bed. My mum passes me my DC trainers I grab them and start to put them on. I notice that my bandages have been removed which is great! My dad then returns to the room looking happier than I've ever seen him.

"Come on son, you're our responsibility now." He says as he holds the door open for us.

I stand up and follow my mum and Piper to the door. My dad puts his arms over my shoulders and pulls me towards him as we make our way out of the hospital.

Chapter 15

Learn Control

"What if?" I think to myself as I lay on my bed.

I sit up and look over to my wardrobe as I have a mirror on the door. I swing my legs off the bed and stand up.

"Would it work?" I mutter to myself walking over to the wardrobe.

I stand in front of the mirror then sit down in front of it. I look at my reflection looking back at me. Slowly I take a deep breath and exhale.

"Come on Lockie! You can do this!" I whisper as I close my eyes.

I begin to think of the worst things. Killian killing mum and dad, his attempt to kill me, Trey and Deccan betraying me. I think of everything possible to piss me off. Suddenly I find my body burning up, I begin to shake.

"Control it..." I mumble whilst clenching my fists.

I quickly stand up, I begin to feel sick and the strange headache begin to fire up. I open my eyes to look in the mirror, it's the other me.

"You need to let the anger overtake you." My reflection says to me with an eerie smile.

"I want to be in control!" I growl.

Then it hits me. I feel the rage rushing through my body as if it's my fuel. It feels amazing. I begin to laugh then I get an idea... I can use this towards Trey and Deccan. I smile at the thought of hurting them, it feels like great revenge.

"Lockie? Can you come downstairs we want to discuss some things with you?" My mum says from behind the door.

I try to snap back to reality but I can't. I grab my head and collapse to the floor and begin to growl in anger.

"Let... me... go..." I splutter as I clench my hair and head butt the floor.

"It's too late Lockie; You shouldn't have thought about trying to control it." A creepy voice says to me.

"Get out my head!" I scream.

My dad throws my door open and rushes into me. He kneels next to me.

"Get away from me!" I yell as I wrap my arms behind my head on the floor.

"Breathe..." He says softly.

"I... can't!" I snap at him as I begin head butting the floor.

"Listen to me, follow what I say..." He continues.

"Don't listen to them! They want to stop this!" The creepy voice hisses.

"I can do it myself! I need to gain control!" I shout.

My dad puts his hand on my back. But the urge, the anger was too much to control. Suddenly I grab my dad's arm, I quickly throw myself up and twist his arm. He screams in pain as I twist it behind his back.

"Lockie! Stop!" My mum cries.

I want to stop but I want to hurt him also. Before I know what is happening, Quin rushes into the room and clicks his fingers; then I pass out.

I awoke on the couch in the living room. My mum, Piper, Quin, and my dad are all sitting and at the same time talking. I look at my dad; his arm was in a sling.

"What... happened?" I groan as I sit up holding my head.

"You're so incompetent!" Quin snaps.

"What? What do you mean?" I mumble as I place my feet onto the floor.

"You think you can control this? It's impossible!" He yells.

"It's ok Quin. He must have done it to try and keep us safe." My mum reassures.

"You could have been killed!" He continues to yell.

I look at my dad then back at Quin. I have a feeling I did that to him.

"I... just wanted to control the anger. To prevent what happened to my parents." I splutter as I rub my face.

"And look how that turned out Lockie!" Quin shouts as he steps towards me.

"What would have happened if I didn't run in and intervene?" He asks whilst glaring at me.

"I... I don't know..." I stutter as I begin to cry.

"You're dangerous! And for you and Thea... how could you be so stupid to bring him home?" He continues.

I stand up and head to the door to go out. Quin quickly grabs my arm.

"You're going nowhere." He roars as he pulls me away.

The forceful grip and the fact he is screaming at me and putting me down just made me angrier.

"If I was you I would let go of my arm and back off!" I bark as I yank my arm from his grip.

I grab the door handle and threw the door open with force. I storm out and do the same with the front door and I walk down the path.

"Lockie! Get back in!" My dad shouts to me.

"Lockie! This isn't you, come back!" My mum cries.

I throw my hood up and run down the drive onto the street.

I sit on the bench at the skate park. No one is around and it's quiet. All I can keep thinking about is control. I want to control this condition and not let it control me. I keep thinking of ways around it. The more I think it becomes clear that I may need to make myself go into these rage frenzy's to learn how to get out. Then the next step is to learn how to prevent one and then moving onto how to control it.

"Attempt 2.," I say to myself as I stand from the bench.

I take a deep breath and think of something that will instantly put me into a raging frenzy. The mental institute. Just the thought of the name triggered me.

"Come to our side." The creepy voice says again.

I smile. Each frenzy I go into the more amazing the feeling is. It's like the high that I have craved with the drugs. The rush, the adrenaline, my heart racing.

"Yes, I will join you." I chuckle.

I look ahead and see a figure stands watching. The figure is wearing all black and have their hood up.

"Kil? Is that you bro?" I smile as I begin to walk in their direction.

The closer I got the more I notice his big smile. It is Killian. I stop in front of him and give a smile back.

"So? Have you finish your murder spree today?" I ask.

"Lockie? Is it you?" He says as his smile got bigger.

"Yes, it's me," I say.

Killian stands and stares. He thought I was dead. He was told I was dead.

"No! It can't be possible!" He growls as he grabs his head.

"Yes, it is. I survived." I smile.

He steps back. He let go of his head then fled. I know now, he can't and won't hurt me. I start to try and snapback. I grab my head and fall onto my knees.

"I'm... not... him..." I splutter as the headache becomes more unbearable.

I try to think of good things. Callie... I promise her I will stay sane. My family... they want to help me. The headache begins to ease and I slowly let go of my head. I start to take deep breaths; I begin to feel normal again.

"It worked..." I whisper to myself.

I begin to laugh and run to the park exit. I can't believe it worked!

I open the door to my house and notice everyone is still in the living room.

"I can control it!" I yell as I run into the living room.

Everyone looks at me instantly. They don't look happy about me disappearing as I did.

"That's great..." My dad mumbles as he sits down on the chair.

"Why aren't you all happy about it?" I ask.

"You don't know the seriousness of it. If you can put yourself into a rage frenzy you could hurt your family if you can't snap out of it." Quin explains.

"I want to control it to keep my family safe!" I yell.

"You could make yourself worse! We don't know the ins and outs of it Lockie!" Quin yells back.

"Why are you acting like you know it all? You have no idea! All you do for a living is spiritual, hypnotism shit!" I snap.

"I know a lot more than you." He smirks.

It starts again I am going into a raging frenzy. I just want to punch him in the face.

"Enlighten us than on your knowledge," I growl.

"Like how I know you're going into a raging frenzy now?" He replies with a smile.

"I hope I am so I can permanently shut you up!" I continue.

Quin nods to my mum, dad, and Piper. They walk into the kitchen and close the door behind them.

"Show me your worst," Quin suggests.

I smile and feel tears roll down my face. I feel more enraged than I ever have with a raging frenzy.

"I didn't realize you were in phase 3 Lockie. You do know them aren't tears but blood?" He explains.

"I... don't... care!" I growl as my fists began to shake.

"Do you not want to know what your body goes through during a major rage frenzy?" He asks followed with a smirk.

I just wait until the right moment to take him out. The more he talks the angrier I got. Even though I don't realize it was possible.

"Your brain goes into temporary insane/psychopath mode as it mimics the toxins that are released when a person does completely snap." He explains.

"The more I explain the angrier you will become. Because you're a scared little boy who doesn't want to turn into what your brother is... a monster." He continues followed with a smile.

"You have no idea what I could be capable of! And I'm not a scared little boy!" I growl.

I feel my nose bleed and my ears. I start to become scared, but I'm not admitting it or showing it. My body hit the boiling point, I feel I have hit the peak with my anger.

"You are a scared little boy Lockie. You've always been so sweet and scared of your shadow until you got your diagnosis. Now you're starting to become what your brother is." He adds.

"Shut up! Shut up! SHUT UP!" I scream as I cover my ears.

My dad steps into the living room behind me.

"Shut him up! Wipe that smile from his face!" The creepy voice hisses.

I throw myself onto Quin and begin to punch him over and over again uncontrollably. My mum and Piper rush in screaming as my dad tries to grab me off Quin. I can see how bad the injuries are that I have inflicted but I can't stop.

"Lockie stop!" My mum cries.

My dad manages to grab the back of my hoodie and pulls me away. I fell on the floor onto my back. I begin panting from the punches I swung then I pass out.

I wake up in bed. I climb out and walk to my wardrobe door. I notice the blood all over my face, I look down at my hands which are also covered in blood. I instantly scream at the top of my lungs and begin to cry. My mum rushes into my bedroom.

"What's the matter, sweetheart?" She panics.

"Who's is this blood? Why do I have blood all over me?" I cry.

I begin to have a panic attack and collapse to the floor. My mum puts her arm around me.

"I'll run you a shower sweetheart and we'll talk." She whispers as she stands and walks out of the bedroom.

What have I done? Who's is this blood? I can't stop thinking about the loss of control to the point I hurt someone. My mum opens my door.

"Shower is running now." She smiles as she shut the door slightly behind her.

I stand up and head to my door. I open it and look down the landing, she has gone. I turn left into the bathroom and close the door behind me. I begin to get undressed by removing my t-shirt first. I look into the mirror properly and realize I have blood in the whites of my eyes. I shake my head and continue to take my jeans off and so on. I step into the shower and begin to wash all the blood off me. I wash my hair then turn the shower off. I then get out and get a towel on and open the door. Piper stands and stares at me.

"What?" I ask.

"Nothing..." She says as she walks past me.

I watch her walk downstairs. She turns to look at me again as she walks down. The look she kept giving me was suspicious. I walk into my bedroom and close the door so I can get dressed.

Chapter 16

I Don't Know Who I Am Anymore

I walk into the kitchen and see my dad and two of his colleagues behind him. My mum and Piper are sitting at the table silently.

"What's going on?" I ask whilst looking at everyone.

"Quin says he wants to file charges." My dad says disappointingly.

"For what?" I ask.

"You beat him to a pulp Lockie. He's in hospital." Piper interrupts.

That can't be true! How did that even happen if I've been at home? Why did my mum not react to the blood all over me? Something isn't adding up.

"So I'm going to prison?" I ask as I begin to get upset.

"I've convinced the judge for house arrest. My colleagues here are going to fit an electronic tag to your ankle. You have to obey curfews only which is 8 pm. It also has GPS so we know where you are at all times." He explains.

I nod at sit down on the dining room chair. I hold my leg out for the officer to put it on.

"It's ok Dom you don't need to restrain him." My dad says to the other colleague behind him.

The other colleague bends down and begins to fit the tag to my ankle. Then he stands up and smiles at me.

"There is no way of removing it. If it is somehow removed, you will be arrested and sent to the Asylum immediately." My dad continues.

I nod then stand from the chair and go to head upstairs.

I lay on my bed and try to remember what happened. That doesn't sound like something I can be capable of. I'm not that type of person. Suddenly there was a knock at my door.

"Come in," I shout.

Piper walks in and closes the door behind her quietly. I look at her confused. She never comes into my bedroom.

"You're so like your brother." She says quietly.

"Thanks... Like I wanted to hear that." I grumble as I sit up.

"It's not a bad thing..." She adds with a smile.

"Of course it is! I'm a psychopath in the making." I splutter.

She walks over to my bed and sits down next to me. She smiles again and places her hand on my leg. She leans over to my ear.

"I like the danger, I like bad boys." She whispers into my ear whilst rubbing her hand up and down my thigh.

Slowly she sits back and bites her lip. This is messed up. How can I be getting it up from this when she is supposed to be my adopted sister! Piper leans in and kissed me, she then sits back slightly to see what my reaction is... I like it. I lean to kiss her. I feel her hand going under my t-shirt feeling my abdomen slowly sliding up to my chest. I put my hand up the back of her top to her bra, I unclasp it with my fingers. She stops kissing me and smiles. I wink at her. She pulls my t-shirt off and look at me up and down.

"So that was the reason you looked at me the way you did after my shower," I whisper with a smile.

She chuckles and nods. I grab her top and take it off over her head. I lay down in my bed as she begins to unfasten my jeans. I can't believe what I'm doing. It feels wrong... but I love it.

I lay in bed with Piper next to me. I wrap my arms around her and she snuggles into my shoulder.

"Lockie! Callie is here!" My mum shouts from downstairs.

My heart stops. Piper quickly climbs out of my bed and grabs her clothes. We hear the footsteps coming up the stairs.

"Piper! Just hide! Leave your clothes!" I whisper.

She drops her clothes and runs to my wardrobe and climbs in.

Knock, knock

"Yeah?" I shout.

Callie opens the door. I hold the covers up to my neck.

"Oh, sorry. Is it a bad time?" She chuckles.

"Erm... I do need to get dressed if you don't mind?" I ask with a smile.

Callie smirks and turns to face the door. I grab my clothes from the end of my bed and get dressed as quickly as I can.

"Do you want to go out?" I ask as I hop around getting my socks on.

"I was going to suggest a movie here or something. Just to limit your out time." She suggests.

"Err... oh..." I stutter.

"Is that not a good idea?" She asks.

I put my boxers on then quickly put my feet into my jeans and stand up. I jump up and down to pull them up. Then Callie turns to look at me. I freeze.

"I'm not finished yet..." I laugh as I fastened my jeans.

She blushes as she looked at my body.

"Oh! Yeah, I'll turn back around..." She smiles as she faces my door again.

I shake my head and smile as I grab my t-shirt from my bed. I have the feeling that she has turned around again. I turn to look at her. Her face says it all. She has seen the scratches on my back from Piper.

"I take it you had company then?" She asks whilst trying to keep back the tears.

"Callie... It's not what you think..." I splutter as I quickly threw my t-shirt over my head.

"I understand Lockie. Like I said, I know I'm not your type so why not just say that to me?" She asks.

"I'm not ready for a relationship! Jesus!" I snap.

I storm over to my shoe rack and grab my vans and begin to put them on.

"You're not ready for a relationship but yet you're having sex with someone else?" She yells.

"Will you shut up yelling that!" I hiss as I continue to tie my laces.

"Why? Scared your parents will judge you for being a man slag?" She barks as she walks towards me.

"Have you heard yourself? You sound like an obsessed lunatic!" I continue.

I stand up from tying my laces... I need a jacket out of my wardrobe. Crap...

"What's happening to you? You would never treat anyone like this! You would never use or lead someone on!" She yells.

"Oh Callie, shut up!" I mumble as I open my wardrobe slightly.

Piper sits there with one of my hoodies on. I smile at her as I grab one from a hanger.

"Suits you..." I whisper to her followed by a wink.

She points in Callie's direction then did the 'she's loopy' sign. I chuckle, she smiles.

"Are you talking to yourself?" Callie pipes up.

I close the wardrobe and put my hoodie on whilst looking at Callie in silence. I then walk past her and open my bedroom door.

"Ladies first..." I say with a sarcastic smile.

"Jerk." She spits.

I roll my eyes and close the door behind us to allow Piper to get dressed and out of my room.

We walk through the park. Callie hasn't spoken to me since we left. Maybe she is right... maybe she isn't my type.

"So is this walk going to be just complete silence?" I ask as I turn to look at her.

She stops and turns to me.

"Tell me..." She says.

"What? If I still like you?" I ask raising my eyebrow.

"Yes." She says bluntly.

"I think it's more as a friend Callie..." I reply.

She begins to cry. I hate it when she cries.

"I'm sorry. I don't know where my head is at..." I add.

Suddenly she puts her hands on my cheeks and kisses me. But it doesn't feel right. I gently push her off me.

"Callie! Are you not taking in what I'm saying?" I bark as I step back.

"What have I done to deserve this?" She cries.

"It's not you!" I continue.

I begin to walk away. I can't do this. She can't take no for an answer.

"Come to mine then. We can talk properly." She sniffs.

"No," I say as I continue to walk off.

"Lockie!" She cried.

I had to walk away. I can't take it how desperate she is for me. Begging and arguing with me. I don't need it with what's going on at the moment.

I get back home and head straight to the kitchen. My mum and Piper sit on their laptops. I smile at Piper as I walk past her.

"So how did it go with Callie? She seems like a lovely girl." My mum asks.

"She's just a friend mum," I reply.

Piper looks at me again and did a shy smile then looks back at her laptop.

"But you seem close..." My mum adds.

I grab my phone and text, Piper, to meet me in her room I can't help but smile.

"I know mum, but we're just friends," I repeat.

Piper texts back. "I'm going to a party tonight..."

I look at her and she looks at me and shrugs. Then my mum takes her glasses off and turns to me.

"You look happy, who are you chatting to?" She asks with a smile.

My heart stopped. Piper continues on her laptop.

"No one," I say quickly.

My mum chuckles to herself and put her glasses back on and continues with her work.

"If you say so…" She says as she smiles.

I text Piper again. "Can I not join?"

She looks at me then shot her eyes at mum and back at me.

I text her again. "See you upstairs then."

I grab a can of cola from the fridge and head upstairs to my room. I close my door and sit at my desk. I open my laptop and log in to social media. I have unread messages from Trey and Deccan. I open Trey's messages.

"I can't believe you did that to my dad! You're an absolute crazy freak."

I sigh and shut the messages. I open Deccan's which is a photo of him and Callie. Callie kissing him on the cheek and him holding a bottle of lager. Yeah… that's not going to bother me. Suddenly Piper opens my door and walks in shutting it quietly behind her.

"Would it be wise you coming to the spring break party?" She asks.

"Why?" I ask with a smile.

"What do I tell my friends? I've told them you're my brother…" She begins to stress.

"Tell them you lied…" I chuckle.

She shakes her head and smiles. She walks over to me and wraps her arms around me whilst I sit at my desk.

"What about your ankle tag?" She asks.

"Tell mum and dad to make an exception for my first spring break party and that I will be safe with you?" I laugh.

"Great thinking batman. I'll call dad now, come into my room soon so we can get ready." She continues as she walks out of my bedroom.

I sit back and smiles. I'm looking forward to this!

I get to Piper's room and open the door. I close it quietly behind me. She is sitting doing her makeup.

"What did dad says?" I ask as I sit on her bed.

"You can go as long as I don't let you out of my sight." She smiles.

I stand up and hug her.

"Thank you," I whisper.

"Come on, let's get you dressed!" She says with a big smile.

We go to my room, Piper brings her comb and straighteners with her.

"Go on I trust you." I laugh.

She chuckles as she lays the straighteners and comb onto my desk as she passes. She opens my wardrobe and picks a band hoodie. She throws it to me on the bed. She then walks over to my drawers and opens the top one with all my t-shirts in. She grabs a plain white one throws it to me then runs back to my wardrobe and unhooks a blue and black cheered shirt. She also throws that at me.

"Stuff that I never wear?" I question.

"Clothes that will make all the ladies jealous!" She giggles.

She then opens my second drawer and grabs my dark blue wash look skinny jeans. Also throws them at me. She shuts the drawer and stares at my shoe rack.

"My black and blue DC's!" I point out.

She turns and smiles, then throws them at me.

"Ok, get dressed so I can do your hair!" She says excitedly.

I get dressed and sit on my chair at my desk. She grabs the brown hair spray and her comb. She splits my fringe in 2 straightens it then sprays the bottom part brown. She then straightens the top part and put it on top of the brown. She then straightens the rest of my hair and backcombs the roots. She then gives me her mirror.

"You look different with piercings and your hair like that." She smiles.

I look into the mirror. I do look different... I don't look recognizable.

"You need to do my hair more often." I laugh.

She leaves to put her stuff back in her room and I stand up and head to the landing to wait for her. She comes out of her room and takes a selfie of us, then we head downstairs to leave for the party.

Chapter 17

The New Me

We arrive at the party. Everyone is already there. I can't help but smile, I feel like a normal teenager again.

"Let's go then!" Piper says as she grabs my hand and drags me inside.

We get inside where we are welcomed by Piper's best friend.

"Hey!" She says as she hugs Piper.

"I didn't know you were bringing a plus one." She says with a smile.

"Sorry, is it ok?" Piper asks.

"Of course! He's hot..." Her friend says.

I blush and turn to look around. I'm going to be shown off here.

"Hey! He's mine!" Piper laughs.

Her friend grabs her phone and puts her arm around me. Piper does the same. They both lean in to kiss me on the cheeks and I pull a scrunched up face with my tongue out. Her friend and Piper let go and we look at the photo.

"Fit!" Her friend laughs.

We watch as she puts it onto social media. Piper grabs my hand and hugs my arm.

"We have alcohol in the kitchen if you want a drink?" Her friend says.

"Sure let's get a drink, Lockie," Piper says happily as she drags me to the kitchen.

She opens a bottle of vodka and pours it into two cups. She then adds the punch from the bowl into the cups. She grabs a cup and passes it to me then grabs one for herself.

"To us!" She shouts over the music.

"To us!" I repeat.

We linked arms and drank our drinks all in one. We then throw them down onto the bar.

"Wow! That was strong!" I laugh.

"I don't make weak drinks!" She shouts again followed by a laugh.

She then pours us another vodka punch. I turn around and see Trey, Deccan, and Callie behind me. They haven't noticed me.

"Fake friends alert!" I shout to Piper.

She turns around and passes me my drink. She looks over to them and took a sips of her drink.

"Wannabes." She laughs.

Callie looks over in our direction. She doesn't even click that it's me staring back. I knock back another mouthful of drink. And head out of the kitchen to the balcony. Piper follows me.

"So what do you think so far?" She asks.

"It's great! I love it." I say with a smile.

I grab my cigarettes from my back pocket and light one up. Piper begins to dither.

"Here, have my hoodie," I say as I takes it off.

I place it over her and wrap my arm around her. I take a toke of my cigarette then look inside and notice Callie is watching with Deccan.

"I think they know it's you now." Piper chuckles.

I shrug and quickly smoke the rest of my cigarette and threw it over the balcony. We walk back in then Deccan stops me.

"Lockie? Is that you?" Deccan asks.

Callie and Trey were stood behind him. Piper grabs my hand.

"Ignore the jerks. If they keep pestering us, I'll get them booted." She growls at them as she pulls me away.

We stand with Piper's friends who are happy to take photos and hug me. I begin to get annoyed with the fact that I am being watched by Callie, Deccan, and Trey.

"I'll be back in a minute. I need to take a leak." I say to Piper.

She nods then kisses me. I head off to the front of the house. I know I will get followed, that's what I want.

"Hey, dick weed!" Trey yells at me.

I stop, sigh and turn around.

"Why are you stalking me?" I yell.

"Why? You've stabbed us all in the back Lockie!" Trey continues.

"Me? Who was the one who made me overdose on drugs? Oh yeah, it was you Deccan! Who was the one who told your dad to wipe all recent memories? Oh yeah, it was you, Callie! Lastly... Who was the one who always got me into trouble? Oh, that would be you!" I yell at them.

They all stood in shock as they thought about it. I began pacing up and down the yard to keep myself sane.

"You used Callie though..." Deccan adds.

"I didn't! I didn't promise anything!" I screamed at him.

"You made me promise to wait for you after your diagnosis settles." Callie points out.

"Just leave me alone!" I yell as I head back into the house.

Trey grabs my arm. I stop and turn around to face him.

"I would let go if I was you. I'm trying not to go into a rage frenzy and you're not helping." I growl.

"What so you can go and shag your new bird?" He snaps.

"Already have and happily do it again." I splutter as I yank my arm from his grip.

As I begin heading back into the house Piper stands at the door and waits for me. She knows by the look on my face what has happened.

"Go and get a drink from the kitchen. Amy will boot them." She says to me.

Piper and Amy walkout to Trey, Deccan, and Callie.

"Go home," Amy shouts bluntly.

"Why?" Trey snaps.

"One, you have an attitude problem, and two, you're causing problems. I don't like drama!" She yells.

"And for you pretty face, stay away from my boyfriend!" Piper hisses as she points to Callie.

"Oh! Is she trying to steal your bf?" Amy says with a smirk.

Callie begins to cry.

"Aww darling, he's not your type! You're like a four and he's like... ten!" Amy laughs with Piper.

"No need to be bitches!" Deccan snaps.

"We're just stating facts. Why don't you dip it with her?" Piper laughs.

Trey grabs Callie and Deccan and drags them away.

"Goodbye low lives!" Amy giggles as she links Piper.

I have had 10 drinks; it's hit me bad. Piper appears next to me.

"Wow... how many drinks have you knocked back since I've been gone?" She giggles.

"Lost... count..." I slur.

"Come on upstairs you need a lie-down," Piper says as she grabs my hand.

We get into the spare room. She shuts the door behind us and locks it. I turn to look at her.

"Come here," I say.

Piper smiles and walks over to me. I put my arms around her and slowly unzip her dress.

"Let's do it again." I smile.

She nods and pushes me onto the bed. We get undressed and begin kissing.

Piper wakes me up. She let me sleep for a bit to try and simmer down on being too drunk.

"Come on sleepy head we can have another hour here then head home." She smiles.

I climb out of the bed and get dressed. Piper stands in front of me and fixes my hair as I tie my laces on my DC's. I sit up and she gives me her hand. I grab her hand and we head back downstairs.

We get there and it starts again. All her friends taking selfies of us. Piper joins in with taking photos of us too. We continue to have some more drinks until it was time to head home.

I get home and stumble to my bedroom. Piper giggles behind me quietly. I get to my door and push it open and stumble over to my bed and fall forwards onto it.

"You really cannot handle alcohol." Piper snickers.

"I don't care," I mumble into my bed.

Piper closes my door and begins to get me undressed for bed.

"Stay with me?" I ask.

"I can't. Mum and dad will end up getting an idea." She whispers as she begins to pull my jeans off.

"Just tonight... I'm so drunk..." I mumble.

She giggles again. I sit on the bed properly and take my top and shirt off.

"Tell them you stayed on the floor you wanted to make sure I was fine." I continue.

"Fine..." She whispers.

I climb into bed and wait for Piper to get ready for bed herself. But before she gets into bed I fall asleep.

"Piper! Lockie!" My mum panics as she slams a door.

I wake and find Piper is asleep on the floor with blankets. My mum opens my bedroom door and breathes a sigh of relief.

"You gave me a heart attack!" She says as she tries to regain her breath.

"Sorry..." I mumble as I rub my head.

"Why is Piper in here?" She asks.

"I got drunk... very drunk... she must have stayed in here with me to make sure I was fine," I explain as I look down at her on the floor sleeping peacefully.

"That's our Piper for you. Very caring." My mum says with a smile.

"I'll leave you to it. I'll make a fry up for breakfast you will need greasy food in you." She laughs as she closes the door.

I climb out of bed and lay next to Piper on the floor. I pull some of the blankets over me and wrap my arm around her.

"Wake up lazy," I whisper in her ear.

She opens her eyes slightly and turns to look at me then smiles.

"You smell so bad of alcohol." She says followed by a giggle.

"Oh thanks, that's very romantic." I chuckle.

"We going downstairs?" She asks.

I nod and roll over. I pull myself up using my bed then walk over to the drawers for some clothes.

"Do you work out?" She asks as she sits up.

"Sometimes. Just sit-ups and pull-ups when I feel like it why?" I ask as I grab a t-shirt from my drawer.

"I can see it. If you do it more your abs would be more visible." She says with a wink.

I smile and throw my t-shirt over my head. I go into my next drawer for my shorts.

"I have no one to impress. I was doing it for myself." I laugh as I begin to get my shorts on.

"Make you a deal... If you do a hard-core work out next few weeks we will make ourselves official..." She says with a wink.

It felt wrong just thinking about being in a relationship with Piper but what we've done together so far made it feel like it will be worth it.

"Deal." I smile.

I grab my socks and vans and sit down on my chair and put them on.

"Why do we need to be classed as brother and sister? We aren't even related by blood!" She grumbles.

"Nothing is stopping us. We're not officially related so it's not wrong." I explain as I tuck my laces into my vans.

Piper smiles and stands up. I head to my door and open it. Piper nods and goes out first.

We get downstairs into the kitchen. Mum is cooking as usual and dad is sat reading the newspaper. Piper sits down and I walk to the fridge for a drink.

"It was nice of you to take Lockie with you last night. Even nicer you stayed with him to make sure he was ok in the night." My mum says as she cooks breakfast on the stove.

"It's not a problem. Anything for my little brother." She smiles as she takes a sip of orange juice from her glass.

I grab my phone and text Callie, Deccan, and Trey. I have to apologize for last night. I feel bad, yeah they stabbed me in the back but I did it to them too.

"Breakfast is ready." My mum says as she places everything on the table.

I sigh and put my phone back in my pocket. I don't think I'll be forgiven for what happened.

Chapter 18

It's Too Late

It's been 2 months. My rage frenzy's have been under control I've learned how to control it with the help of Piper. I've worked out, been to the skate park, change my image. I've done everything to better myself without being betrayed by people. Spring break is over and school is back on.

"Piper! Come on we are going to be late!" I shout upstairs.

"I'm ready! One minute!" She shouts back.

My dad walks into the hallway. He grabs his keys and coat.

"Do you want me to drop you both off?" He asks as he put his coat on.

"Please. I don't know why she's taking so long." I explain as I grab my bag from the floor.

"Piper!" My dad yells.

Suddenly she comes running downstairs whilst trying to shuffle her bag onto her shoulder.

"Ready!" She says as she pants.

My dad shakes his head and opens the door. We head to the car and get in.

"Any news on Killian yet?" Piper asks.

"Just gory murders and patterns every week. Just can't get there quick enough." He explains.

I roll my eyes and put my belt on. Piper does the same then looks at me.

"I like your hair like that, suits you." She says with a smile.

My hair is still blonde but with lighter highlights, black in my fringe, and I've kept the style Piper did by backcombing it and my fringe. I've still got my piercings but I have officially got a real stretcher in my ear instead of the fake one.

We arrive at school and wave dad off for work. We head towards to entrance to meet Piper's friends who are sitting on the wall.

"Hey, guys!" She says as she hugs her best friend.

"You look amazing!" Amy says as she hugs Piper.

I walk over to the guys and gave them a bro hug. Everything is going great.

"You're looking like a beast bro!" Cam says.

"Thanks, man! Enjoyed working out over the spring break." I smile.

I glance over to the trees and see Trey, Deccan, and Callie. I feel I need to go over and try and apologize again. It's been long enough.

"I'll be back in a minute," I say as I jog over to the tree.

I slowly approach them. They were happily talking to each other. I stand behind Callie and tap her on the shoulder. She turns around and looks at me. Trey and Deccan roll their eyes and walk away.

"I'm sorry. I was a jerk and I took you for granted." I say.

"I can't just forgive you that easily," Callie says as she looks to the floor.

"How about we hang out at yours tonight? Talk and sort things out. Just us two." I suggest with a smile.

Callie looks up at me. I can see that she wants to smile but she is trying to be stubborn.

"Sure. Meet me at mine after school." She says then heads over to Trey and Deccan.

I watch then begin to step back. I turn and head back to the group.

School finishes and we walk down the corridor to the entrance. Piper links onto me. I casually walk with my hands in my jeans pockets. Everyone is laughing and smiling. I glance over to the lockers and see Callie stood with Trey and Deccan talking. I have a bad idea about tonight.

"Cheer up!" Amy says as she nudges me.

"I am!" I laugh.

We get to the entrance and wait for the buses with everyone else. It didn't take long for Callie, Trey, and Deccan to walk out of school and head home. I wait with everyone until they leave as it will give time for Callie to get home.

Me and Piper are almost home then I stop at the bottom of the street. She stops as soon as I did.

"What's up?" She asks.

"I'm just going to head off to the skate park for a while. I'll see you back at home." I explain.

She nods and continues to walk us to our street. I continue towards Callie's.

It didn't take long for me to get to hers. She was at the front waiting for me.

"Hey..." I say.

"Hey..." She says back.

I hug her. I think this will be the best thing to show she can trust me. Callie then wraps her arms around me and begins to cry. I slowly lean back to look at her.

"Why are you crying?" I ask.

"Because I didn't think you would come back." She sniffs.

I smile and grab her hand.

"I made you make a promise. I never go back on those." I smile.

Callie smiles back then leads the way to hers.

We get to her bedroom and I sit down on her bed. She throws her bag onto the floor then walks over to me.

"So what do you want to talk about?" She asks.

I place my hand onto her cheek and gently kiss her on her lips. She pulls away and looks at me in shock.

"Sorry..." I say.

"No... Carry on..." She says with a smile.

I smile back and then continue to kiss her. I place my hand on her thigh and begin to stroke my hand inwards. She then puts her hand on my abdomen and gently begins to stroke. She stops kissing me.

"Didn't think you were the person to work out?" She giggles.

"Needed something to take my mind off my diagnosis." I smile.

She lifts my t-shirt off over my head then she takes her top off.

"Are you sure about this?" I ask.

"Yeah, I trust you." She says with a smile.

We continue to kiss and lay on the bed. She unfastens my jeans and I unfasten hers.

Well, this was easy...

It gets to 7 pm. I leave Callie's to head home. I'm going to get into trouble as I'm past my curfew for this stupid tag. I take a short cut down the dark walkway path. Cutting this way will get me home for 7:10 pm. Suddenly I feel like I am being followed. I stop and turn around to look behind me. No one is there. I shake my head and continue to get home. Just as I get to the turning to get off the path someone grabs me from behind and throws my hood over my head. I struggle as much as I can but it is no use they have a great grip on me. I can't see it nor escape.

"Let me go!" I scream as I continue to kick out.

Before I know it they put a cloth over my nose and mouth and I pass out.

I wake up cuffed to a bed in an old and broken house. I try to pull my arms and my legs but it is no use. I've been kidnapped.

"Whoever you are you will get caught! I have a tag from the police that has GPS!" I scream.

Suddenly someone in all black appear. Holding a knife.

"Killian?" I ask.

He begins to laugh. He places the knife blade onto my arm then look at me.

"What are you doing?" I yell as I try to break free again.

"I need you to join me." He smiles.

He then presses the blade into my arm and makes a deep slice. I scream in agony. He laughs then moves the blade and repeats it again several times. The pain is excruciating, unbearable!

"Please stop!" I cry.

He ignores me and continues to keep gashing my arm. He moves to my other arm and does the same. I can't stand it, I just want to die!

"Just kill me already!" I scream.

But I don't think that's what he wants.

It feels like I've been here for a week. I can't process the torture and the pain any more. I think I will be mentally beyond repair. Suddenly Killian appears again, he shows me he has my phone. I have over 200 missed calls and 100 voice mails. He begins playing the voice mails as he walks over to continue my torture.

All I can hear was people crying, worrying, begging me to go home. Message after message it hurts me. Killian then grabs a bottle with liquid in it. I try to take deep breaths through the pain he has already inflicted on me with the gashes.

"This one should do it. You're a hard one to break little brother." He laughs.

The messages continue playing and Killian turns me over on the bed. I cry into the pillow as he re-cuffs my wrists and ankles to the bed bars. Suddenly he pours the liquid all over my back. I instantly begin to scream! The pain gets worse and worse! I hear my skin on my back sizzling, I can smell it. He has poured acid onto my back. I scream so hard that I hear a snap and pass out.

I awake in the trees in the park. It was dark. I stand up and felt my arms. I can no longer feel the pain. I didn't feel right. I scoop my hoodie from the leaves on the floor and put it on. I make my way home.

I walk through the door. I turn to look in the mirror I have streaks of blood from my eyes and my nose had been bleeding. I have hit a raging frenzy. Suddenly my dad opens the door.

"Oh my god! Lockie!" He yells as he hugs me.

He pulls away and looks at his shirt. The blood from my wounds have soaked through my hoodie onto him.

He quickly leads me into the living room where my mum and Piper are and they rush over to help.

"Take his hoodie off!" Piper panics.

My mum quickly unzips my hoodie to reveal all the slices and the huge burn on my back. I felt like a zombie. I felt nothing.

"We need to get him to a hospital!" My mum screamed.

I stand up and walk towards the kitchen.

"I'm... Fine..." I mumble as I stumble into the kitchen door.

"You're not fine!" Piper shouts as she gently grabs my hand.

I look at her. Then look at her hand holding mine.

"I'm scared," I whisper.

"Why?" She whispers back.

"I can't feel the pain; I can't feel emotion... I think... I've snapped..." I whisper.

Piper begins to cry and she hugs me. I don't know what I can be capable of. I can just decide to kill someone and do all the things Killian does. It's only a matter of time before I go completely psycho.

"Come on let's go to the hospital," Piper whispers as she slowly pulls me to follow her.

My mum grabs her keys and my dad rings his colleagues to meet us there.

I get rushed straight in and treated. A few hours later I was put into my room. My mum and Piper sit next to my bed whilst my dad spoke to his colleagues outside my door. I look to my arm and see I have a cannula for water. I look to my hand and see I have one for blood.

"I'll go and grab something for us all to eat. Stay here with Lockie." My mum says to Piper.

Piper nods then hugs my arm. My mum leaves the room so it was just me and Piper. All I can think about is hunting down Killian and killing him. I begin to laugh as I think about it.

"Lockie? You're scaring me..." Piper whispers.

"I'm just thinking of different ways to kill Killian..." I smile then continues to laugh.

"I thought you liked the bad boys," I whisper.

"I do..." She says.

"Well don't be scared." I smile.

Piper nods and my dad walks in with his colleagues.

"Are you ok to answer questions, Lockie?" My dad asks.

"Sure." I smile.

My dad nods to Piper and they leave the room for me to speak with the police.

"No need to ask questions." I smile.

The two officers look at each other confused. Then they turn to look back at me.

"It was Killian. He did it. He has multiple hideouts that I can give you." I chuckle.

"Sure... are you ok Lockie? After your experience, we wouldn't think you would be acting like this..." One of the officers points out.

"Yeah, I'm great. Just take it on the chin." I smile.

They look at each other again then look at me. The look they give me shows they're worried.

"Ok... here is the pad and paper. Write down what you know." He says as he hands me the pen and pad.

I begin writing it down and they walk to the door and asks my dad and mum to come in. I listen best I can into the conversation.

"I think you should get him tested psychologically." One of the officers suggests to my dad.

"Why? What's he said?" My dad asks quietly.

"He's not acting normal for someone who has been through torture and being kidnapped." He explains.

I look up as I have finished writing.

"Ok, I'll go and speak to a doctor now." My mum whispers.

I force myself to cry. I have to force myself to do it which is the scary part. I need to make myself look like I have been through hell, I have to try and act normal. Act like a normal human.

"I tried acting like everything was ok. I didn't want to show I was weak! I'm in excruciating pain and I can't relive what I saw. I'm sorry!" I cry.

My dad rushes over to me and grabs me for a hug. I scream like it hurt... even though it didn't.

"I'm so sorry son." He panics.

"I can't even hug my son without him screaming in pain!" He yells.

"Sorry boss. We must have over thought it..." One of the officers says.

"Mum I need more painkillers. Please it hurts so much!" I continue to cry.

My mum walks out to find the doctors. My dad leads his colleagues outside. I am left with Piper. She looks at me and watches me carefully. I sit up like nothing happened and wipe the tears away with my bandages on my arms. Then I sigh.

"What the hell was that?" She yells.

"Acting," I say bluntly.

She sits and stares at me in shock. I grab my new phone from the side and begin to unbox it. I look up at Piper who is still staring at me.

"You can stop staring..." I say.

"Have you completely lost it?" She continues.

I pull the phone from the box then look at her and begin to laugh.

"Can you tell?" I laugh.

"This is messed up... you're not going to kill us all are you?" She asks worryingly.

I roll my eyes and lean over the bed to plug the charger in for my new phone. I sit up then smiles at her.

"Have you caused me any pain? Wronged me? Betrayed me?" I ask followed by a smile.

"Err... not as I know of..." She replies.

"Well, there you go. I won't murder you." I laugh then turn the new phone on.

I can tell by her face, what I am saying is scaring her. She can't believe what I am saying. She doesn't need to be scared though, I love her.

The door opens and I quickly throw the phone to Piper and lay back onto the bed and force myself to cry again. I squirm around like I can't cope with the pain.

"It's ok darling the doctor is going to inject some painkillers for you." My mum reassures me.

"Piper? Can you grab the bag of food please?" She asks.

Piper nods and slowly stands up whilst watching me. She then heads over to grab the bag near the door. She slowly brings it over to my mum as she watches how I am acting. I continue to scream and cry then eventually the drugs they gave me made me sleepy.

"Shhh, it's ok sweetheart these will help the pain and allow you to rest." My mum whispers as she strikes my hair.

Before I know it I fall asleep.

A week passes and I still can't feel anything. I've been allowed to go home; I still need checks in the hospital weekly. I may be home but I still feel no pain, no emotion. I stand and stare in the mirror.

"I look like me... but I don't feel like me..." I mumble.

I pull my t-shirt off over my head. The top half of my body is half mummified, the other half not. I make my way to the bathroom, I'm dying to feel something. I close the door behind me and lock it. I open the mirror cupboard and grab the pack of razors then close it. I look in the mirror again. My face is pale, red around my eyes and my pupils are as tiny as a dot. I look physically ill. I open the razors and grab a blade, I take my jeans off and sit at the edge of the bath. I look at the razor blade then my thigh.

"Here goes nothing..." I say.

I put the blade to my thigh and press until I can see blood. Still nothing. I slowly pull the blade down and see my skin open up and the blood flowing from it. Still no pain.

"Why can't I feel anything!" I growl.

I slash and slash multiple gashes onto my thigh. Blood begins to collect on the floor tiles below. I drop the blade and begin to cry in anger. Anger is the only emotion I can feel.

"What the hell is wrong with me?" I yell.

Chapter 19

A Psychopath Pretending

Here I am, faking, still pretending to be normal. My parents still haven't figured out about me and no psychological tests have been done. I've managed to scrape it during hospital visits. I log onto my laptop in my bedroom and begin doing the homework sent from school as I need to stay off a few weeks longer for the healing process. I log onto my social media and see everyone tagging me in posts about me missing. I put a post-up saying 'I'm home and well. Sorry for the scare.'

Knock, knock

"Come in," I shout as I open my homework up.

It's my dad. He shuts the door behind him and sits on my bed.

"You know we are here if you need to talk about your experience? Just to get it off your chest." My dad explains.

"I've already said dad; I don't want to relive what happened. I've blocked it." I say as I begin typing on my laptop.

"You can't bottle it up, Lockie. It will do you more harm than good." He continues.

"Dad. I'm fine." I grumble.

I turn to look at him, he was sitting with his head down, hands together, and his leg shaking.

"Stop worrying about me and just try and catch the prick," I say as I smile at him.

He looks up and smiles.

"Do you need any counseling or anything?" He pushes.

I stop typing. I feel the rage frenzy coming on, it's starting up quicker than it used to. I breathe my way through it.

"Lockie? I'm only trying to help you son." He says.

"How many times... I DON'T NEED HELP!" I yell.

"Just get out..." I growl.

My dad stands up and walks out he didn't say a word. I close my laptop and sit in the middle of my floor. I put my knees up and put my head on my knees and breathe. Slowly the rage subsided.

"Keep it together," I growl.

Slowly I stand up and open my bedroom door to head downstairs. I walk into the living room and everything seems normal.

"How are you feeling darling?" My mum asks.

"Fine," I say bluntly.

"What would you say about going to a meeting tomorrow?" She asks.

I look at her then back at Piper. They've booked me in any way! They're going to end up making me hate them!

"Counselling?" I ask.

"No..." She says as she darts her eyes to my dad who looks back at the TV.

"The more you push me with this the more you're going to push me away. I'm getting pissed off with how you're doing things behind my back!" I snap.

I walk into the kitchen and slam the door behind me. I walk around holding my hands on my head. The whispering, the voices. I begin hitting my head hoping it will stop.

"Shut up! Get out of my head!" I hiss.

I stop. I can hear everyone talking about me. I run over to the door and listen.

"This isn't Lockie at all. He has no ounce of aggression in him." My dad says.

"Even with the rage frenzy's... they were triggered like with Quin saying what he said." My mum admits.

"I've spent a lot of time with Lockie more than anyone in school. This isn't like him at all. He's acting weird." Piper says.

I fling open the kitchen door before she can continue.

"How so?" My mum asks as she glances over to me then looks at Piper.

"Yeah Piper... please share..." I say as I glare at her.

"Have you heard yourself?" Piper yells.

"I'm fine. Why can't you all just get that into your heads!" I yell.

"Piper... he's experienced the unthinkable, of course, he isn't going to be himself." My dad interrupts.

"Just... get off my back. I don't need help or counselling. Let me deal with it my way." I say as I leave the room to go back to my bedroom.

I continue doing my homework on the laptop as well as checking in on social media. I put my headphones on and begin listening to music. Callie then messages me.

"Hope you're ok?"

"Yup never better."

I continue to scroll through to see if I've missed much. I go onto my profile to look at all the spring break photos. I click through them one by one.

"I'd do anything to feel that emotion again." I think to myself.

Suddenly I feel a hand on my shoulder. I quickly throw off my headphones and turn around. It's Piper.

"I wouldn't do that anymore," I say as I turn back to my laptop.

She laughs and wraps her arms around me. She then kisses me on the cheek.

"I'm sorry. I just thought to surprise you." She whispers into my ear.

I smile and spun around on my chair. I pull her to sit on my lap and I turn back to the laptop. I unplug my headphones and let the music play through the speakers.

"I will be me again. Just let me learn how to control myself." I smile.

She nodded then laid her head on my shoulder. I get another message from Callie.

"If you want to go out let me know."

"Sure."

I close the social media page down and open my homework back up.

"Can we not just go out for a walk?" Piper asks.

"Sure," I reply.

She climbs off my lap and runs to my wardrobe and grabs a hoodie each for us. She slowly walks back over and passes me one and begins to put the other on.

We follow the path in the park. I feel like everyone is watching me. I begin to get paranoid. It didn't take long for the voices and whispering to start again. I stop and collapse to the floor holding my head.

"God damn it!" I yell as I put my head on the floor.

"What is it?" Piper asks worryingly.

"This is the only pain I feel and it hurts like hell!" I growl.

Piper knelt next to me and put her arm over my back.

"Breathe." She says.

I begin to take deep breaths. I try to think of positive stuff in hopes it would ease. It worked. Slowly I sit up and look at Piper. Her facial expression shows she is worried and scared. I laugh.

"I'm fine!" I chuckle as I stand up and continues to walk ahead.

"Why don't I believe you when you say that..." She mumbles as she follows me.

We sit on a bench and chill. I can tell Piper wants to know what happened. It is written all over her face.

"You just want the truth don't you?" I ask.

"Yeah, I do. I'm beginning to hate hearing 'I'm fine' when I know you're not." She says.

I sigh and turn to face her on the bench. I grab her hand.

"I'm not going to sugar coat it so tell me if you want me to stop talking," I say.

She nods.

"I went to Callie's and had a chat with her about everything that happened months ago. I want to make up for it. So we chill and talk. I leave late at about 7 pm..." I explain.

"Your curfew." She adds.

"Yeah, I took the shortcut home down the dark walkway. As I was about to turn off someone pulled my hood over my face then I blacked out." I continue.

I can tell she was scared of just saying that.

"I woke up in an old broken down house with my wrists and ankles cuffed to the bed rail. I began shouting and screaming that's when I saw Killian. He says he wanted me to join him and tortured me in multiple ways to get me to snap. He sliced me bit by bit but I kept holding on... until the acid..." I say.

"I don't want to hear anymore..." She interrupts.

"Why?" I ask.

"Because I don't want to get the image of you screaming in so much pain that it caused you to lose your sanity." She explains.

"Now I have to live with hearing voices and whispering day in day out telling me to do the unthinkable that causes a burning headache every time it happens. The fear if I go into a rage frenzy I could kill someone this time. Worst of all I'm trying to feel emotion but I can't." I explain.

Piper let go of my hand and hugs me. She begins to cry then hugs me tighter.

"I'll stand by you. No matter what." She whispers.

"Even if I go psychopath and kill people?" I ask.

"Yeah even then." She replies.

I wrap my arms around her and hug her tightly. I can't believe she just said that.

10 pm and I'm laid in bed, Piper snuggles up to me. All I can think about is trying to get into a rage frenzy and get out of it. I want to feed my urge but control it. I slowly climb out of bed and sit on the floor. I close my eyes and think of someone who has wronged me. Instantly it happens. I slowly stand up and walk over to my mirror. I put my hands at the sides and stare into it.

"Keep control..." I growl.

I let it overtake me bit by bit whilst still keeping control. I began to smile. The feeling was great but I need something to test it out. I go to my bed and wake Piper up. I feel like I want to laugh, I begin to shake. I pause and close my eyes to gain control again.

"Lockie?" She mumbles.

"I... need... revenge..." I splutter.

She quickly sits up and looks at me. I grab my phone to text Trey to meet me at Dead Man's Woods. I start to laugh.

"Lockie... what's happening to you?" She says as she backs away.

I put my phone back in my pocket.

"Shhh, don't be scared." I smile.

She looks at me up and down.

"I'm in control! I feel amazing!" I laugh.

"You can't keep doing this, Lockie. You may be in control now but there is going to be a point it will take over." She states.

"It won't!" I snap.

"All I'm saying is be careful, you may stay that way and not be able to snap out of it. You're already halfway there." She continues.

I roll my eyes and leave my room and run downstairs. I continue to run out of the house onto the street. I'm going to feed this urge for the first time. I know I'm going to enjoy it. I can't control the laughter as I run. I start to sound more and more like Killian, an insane psychopath.

I wait for Trey at the entrance of Dead Man's Woods. I can't wait to get my revenge, and no one will know. Suddenly he turns up on his own. He walks over to me.

"I still hate you, what do you want?" He says bluntly.

I smirk then begin to laugh.

"Well... it's great to know the feeling is mutual." I say with a smile.

Trey looks at me strangely. I grab the rope from my pocket and quickly wrap it around his neck. I grab his phone from his pocket and put it in mine. I then pull it tight so he can't break free from it. I drag him to the floor then drag him into the woods. I watch as he gasps for air and struggles to pull the rope from his throat. The more I watch as I pull him the more I get a rush. I'm enjoying watching him suffer watching him slowly die. I get to the perfect tree and throw the rope over the tree. I pull with all my weight and watch as it drags Trey to the top. The way he wriggles and squirms made me happy. I grab a rock and wrap the rope around it to keep him up in the tree. Suddenly there is a crack and his body goes limp. I close my eyes and begin to bring myself out of the frenzy. Slowly breathing and counting, I do it. I look up and saw his body swinging, I shrug then head home.

I walk into my bedroom and close the door. Piper quickly sits up and looks at me.

"Don't panic I'm fine," I say as I take my hoodie off.

"What have you done?" She asks.

"Nothing, I've just found Trey hanging from a tree in Dead Man's Woods," I reply.

"WHAT?" She yells.

"I know... I can't feel emotion though; you'll have to tell dad." I say.

Piper quickly jumps out of bed then stops and turns to me.

"You did it didn't you?" She asks quietly.

"Maybe I don't know... I can't remember..." I reply.

She shakes her head and runs to mum and dad's bedroom.

"DAD! DAD!" She screams.

I walk in and stand with her. Mum and dad quickly jump up and turn the light on.

"What! What's happened?" He yells.

I put on the acting and force the tears again before Piper can tell him.

"It's Trey!" I cry.

Piper looks at me.

"What's happened, darling?" My mum asks worryingly.

"Me and Piper went for a walk. I know we shouldn't but we went near Dead Man's Woods. Trey's body was hung from a tree." I yell.

I then collapse to the floor and began to scream and cry like it's killing me. Piper knelt next to me crying and held me.

"Grab my phone now!" My dad demands to my mum.

She throws his phone to him and he calls it into work as he walks out of the bedroom. My mum then climbs out of bed and kneels with me and Piper hugging us.

"Right. I've got to go and investigate it. Piper stay in Lockie's room tonight; I want you to make sure he's ok. He's been through enough." My dad explains.

Piper nods then continues to hug me as I continue to cry on the floor.

"Come on darling let's get you into your room." My mum says as she lifts my arm.

My dad also helps to get me off the floor. I stand up and walk out then turn into my bedroom and close the door. I sit on the bed and wait for Piper. It didn't take long for her to walk in.

"You could get caught with this..." She whispers.

"I won't," I whisper back as I wipe the tears.

I get undressed to my boxers and climb into bed. Piper climbs in next to me and cuddles me.

"If deaths look like accidents or suicide I'll get away with it." I smile.

"I'll be your back up anyway, I'm here for you." She says as she hugs me tighter.

I smile and close my eyes.

Chapter 20

What Will Be, Will Be

I sit quietly at the dining table. I twirl my folk on my plate and rest my head on my other hand. Piper sits on her phone scrolling through social media before heading to school.

"I'm so sorry you have to go through this Lockie. This is the worst year for you." My mum says as she places the coffee onto the table.

"When is dad back?" I ask.

"Whenever he's finished dealing with Trey's case sweetheart." She says as she turned back to the stove.

Suddenly we hear the front door close. I sit up and wait for dad to walk through the kitchen. The door opens and he walks in.

"What's the outcome? I want to know!" I beg as tears build up.

My dad looks at me sadly and pulls a chair next to me.

"Suicide son. We've been over it and it and it points to suicide." He says.

I grab him for a hug and cry into his shoulder. He then puts his arms around me and rubs my back.

"I'm sorry son." He whispers.

"Is he going to be ok? Should I still go to school?" Piper asks.

"Up to you honey. I'm going to work soon and I'm sure your dad will be going back in later." She explains.

"I'll stay with Lockie then. Can you ring the school and explain please?" Piper asks.

"Sure honey." My mum replies.

I pull myself from my dad. He rubs my hair and stands up.

"Come on Lockie, let's chill upstairs," Piper suggests.

I nod and follow her upstairs. I'm still crying as I walk up the stairs as mum is in the hallway getting ready to go to work. I have to make it believable.

I sit at my desk and wipe my tears with my sleeve. I open the laptop up and log into social media.

"I'm sorry Lockie but this is messed up..." Piper says as she sits on the bed.

"What is?" I ask as I turn to face her.

"How you can make it so realistic then you're fine like there is a switch..." She continues.

I smile and turn back to the laptop and scroll through the posts. Everyone has already learnt the news of Trey and all the posts were pouring in saying RIP.

"Because I'm a psycho." I chuckle.

I begin to plan my revenge in my head for everyone who has betrayed me. I need to space these murders out so it doesn't become suspicious.

Still weeks after being kidnapped and tortured I'm still a crazy, zero sanity, psycho. I'm beginning to hate living like this. I don't want to live like this, he should have just killed me.

I make my way downstairs; all I have on my mind is 'I want to die'.

"Are you ok sweetheart? You've been quiet for the last few days." My mum asks.

"I suppose," I reply bluntly.

I continue to the kitchen. I pull the chair from the dining table, sit down then place my face onto the table.

"If there is a god, end my suffering. This isn't humane." I say in my head.

My dad walks into the kitchen and grabs the coffee jug. I hear him pouring his coffee.

"I know you don't want me to bring it up again Lockie but, therapy could help." He says as he stirs his coffee.

"I want to die, I don't want help," I mumble into the table.

"I'll look about for a great therapist for you, son." He says as he places his coffee on the table.

I begin to lightly bang my head onto the table, not like I can feel anything anyway.

"Lockie stop it." My mum says as she walks in.

I ignore her and continue to do it a little harder. My dad then throws the kitchen towel under my head. I lift my head and look at him.

"I don't know what Killian did to you but this is not you at all." He snaps

I roll my eyes then drop my head back on the kitchen towel on the table with a thud. I decide to go to my room, I slowly stand up and walk out the kitchen door.

I sit on my bed in my room and look at my calendar on the wall across from me, it's been 3 weeks since Trey's death. The best thing is... no one suspects anything other than suicide.

Knock, Knock

Piper opens my bedroom door and peeps her head in. She looks at me and smiles.

229

"Morning." She says.

"Morning." I smile.

She walks in and shut the door behind her. She sits next to me on the bed and looks at the calendar in front of us.

"3 weeks already?" She asks.

"Yeah…" I reply.

We sit silently and stare at the date. Suddenly…

"Lockie! Deccan and Callie are here!" My mum shouts from the bottom of the stairs.

I quickly jump out of bed and grab whatever clothes out of my drawers. I grab a hoodie from my door and get dressed.

"One minute!" I shout.

Piper sits up in bed and looks at me. She smiles as she watches me get dressed.

"I'll wait until you get home. I'll be in my bedroom." She says.

I nod and head out my door. I rush downstairs to the front door.

"Sorry I slept in," I say as I try to catch my breath.

"It's ok, no rush." Callie smiles.

I sat at the door and grab my doc martens from under the coat rack. I begin to tie my laces.

"Trey didn't have his phone when he was found by police," Deccan says as he looks at me.

"Is that so?" I reply as I stand up.

"Do you not think it's a bit weird?" Callie asks.

I close the front door behind me and stand on the step.

"People can lose phones... plus since it was suicide he probably threw his phone somewhere before he did it," I explain.

"I guess so... I don't understand why he did it..." Callie says as she shook her head.

I grab her hand and gently lift her head with my finger.

"I know it's not nice, we all feel the same about this. But you need to stop overthinking. Nobody knows what's going on in someone's head." I explain.

Callie looked at Deccan and Deccan looked at me.

"Yeah man, you're not wrong." He says.

We head off down the street to go to the cemetery where Trey is buried.

The cemetery is quiet; the only sound was the trees swaying in the breeze. I follow Callie and Deccan as they know where they're going, I don't. I place my hands in my jeans pockets as I walk behind them. I have one problem.

They're full of emotion and I'm here staying back feeling... nothing.

"He's here Lockie." Callie points out.

I slowly approach his headstone and stare. How am I supposed to act? What do I say?

"Dude, it's ok to cry. You don't have to bottle it up." Deccan says as he places his hand on my shoulder.

"We've all cried here," Callie adds as she put her arm around me.

I nod. I force the tears to come through, I didn't want to come across cold-hearted.

"I hate we didn't sort out our friendship before he did it," I say as the tears roll down my cheeks.

"That's understandable. But you were like brothers of course you're going to still be upset over him."

Callie opens her bag and lifts out a small bunch of roses. She places them in front of Trey's headstone.

"Sleep tight Trey." She whispers.

She stands up and tears begin to build up in her eyes. She then walks over to me and hugs me, I wrap my arms around her.

"He's still watching over us," I say as I hug her a little tighter.

"I know." She sniffed and pushes away.

We walk towards the cemetery exit; I still feel nothing. I look at Deccan and Callie; all I can think of is the betrayal. I want my revenge, but who next?

It got to the evening and we are sat watching movies at Deccan's with drinks and junk food. Callie lay on my chest and Deccan slouches in his gamer chair.

'If they're drunk maybe I could do something tonight.' I think with a smile.

"What time are we ending tonight?" I ask.

"Whenever dude." Deccan replies.

I need to plan this carefully and ensure I can get one away from the other. I look at Deccan then look at Callie.

"Want me to walk you home tonight?" I ask Callie.

"Sure! I'd love that." She smiles.

I smile back and gently kiss her on the top of her head. Then I turn to continue watching the movie as I wrap my arms around her.

9 pm and it's dark outside. It's the perfect opportunity to seal their fate. Callie walks out of the bedroom to the bathroom, leaving me and Deccan together.

"Do you want to walk with us to Callie's?" I ask.

"Sure man, we need to watch each other's backs." He mumbles.

I nod and we wait for Callie to come back into the room. I grab my doc martens and put them on, I don't remove my hoodie due to the scaring from Killian. But I never removed my hoodie anyway.

"Are we ready? I'm getting tired." Callie asks.

"Yeah, just tying my laces then we can go," I add.

I finish up tying my laces then we head downstairs. Me and Callie wait by the door whilst Deccan puts his jacket on.

"Why won't you take off your hoodie?" Callie asks.

"You know the answer to the questions, why ask?" I say.

"It shows you're a survivor, a warrior if that." She smiles.

"You don't understand how much I hate my body now do you?" I say.

She just pauses and looks at me, then looks to the floor.

"Are we ready to rumble?" Deccan laughs.

"Sure," Callie says as she opens the front door.

We head off down the drive as Deccan locks up. His parents aren't home much due to their jobs. He pretty much has the house to himself. Deccan meets us at the end of the drive and we head to Callie's.

We stand outside of Callie's and she hugs Deccan first. I have to admit I felt jealous. It didn't take long for her to then turn to me. She wraps her arms around me and I do the same.

"I love you." She whispers.

"You don't mean that you're drunk," I reply.

"I do." She says as she pulls away.

She then puts her hands on my cheeks and kisses me. It only lasted a few seconds then she let go.

"Woo! About time!" Deccan shouts.

"Shhh! It's late!" I hiss.

"See you later guys. Get home safe." She says as she walks into her garden.

Me and Deccan then head down the street back towards his.

"Want to walk down the river way?" He asks.

"Sure, if it's quicker," I reply.

We walk down a dark path surrounded by trees. This can be my opportunity to get revenge on Deccan. I smile as we got closer to the river way.

"Why this way?" I ask.

"It's just quicker." He says.

I keep quiet and we exit onto the river way. We walk along for 5 minutes. Do I need my rage frenzy for something so easy? Before I can think I quietly reach for a rock nearby then I swing and hit Deccan at the side of his head then push him into the river. I throw the rock in with him. I stand and watch the water, there was no struggle, no sound. I've achieved my second revenge. I begin to laugh as I continue down the river way. I feel amazing after that! I want to do more.

"I'm sorry," I say.

"I'm sorry I didn't make it more brutal, more gruesome..." I smirk.

I head back the way we entered the river way and walk back home.

The next day starts normally. I wake up, get dressed, and stay in my room on my laptop. I listen to music through my headphones and do my work for school. I just need to continue and act like I didn't know what happened last night.

Knock, knock

I bop away to the music I'm listening to and check on social media. The door opens my dad enters and sees I'm busy on my laptop. He walks over and taps my shoulder. I turn to look at him and slowly remove my headphones. His colleagues were at my door with my mum and Piper.

"What's going on?" I ask.

My dad looks at everyone and looks back at me.

"What happened after you walked Callie home?" He asks.

"I told Deccan that I'm heading home as I felt tired and said I would meet him later today. We then split ways and I came home... why?" I ask.

My dad sighs and my mum comes into my room and kneels next to me. I look at her and then look back at my dad.

"Dad?" I say.

"We had a report of a body found early this morning in the river. It was Deccan's, Lockie. I'm so sorry son..." He says.

Time to be dramatic again and act distraught.

"What? But I had left him! Why did I leave him?" I cry.

"I know son." My dad replies calmly.

"What happened? Was he murdered? What was it?" I yell.

"We are in the process of finding out, son." My dad explains.

I collapse off my chair and curl up on the floor. I scream and continue to let the tears flow.

"I hate breaking the news to him." My dad whispers to my mum.

Piper walks over and hugs me as I'm still curled up on the floor. My dad leaves with his colleagues and I'm left with my mum and Piper.

A few hours pass and I sit on my bed and stare at my wall. I feel numb, emotionless. I stand up and drag my feet to my drawers. As I grab the drawer handle I look at the scars on my arms.

"If people didn't know any better they would think I self-harm," I mumble as I pull open the drawer.

I grab a clean t-shirt and throw it onto my bed. I close the drawer with my hip and walk to my wardrobe. I take my t-shirt off and look at the scars all over my torso. Piper opens the bedroom door and looks at me as she quietly closes it.

"Are you ok?" She asks.

"What do you think?" I reply.

She sighs and heads over to me. She wraps her arms around me.

"It's not about how your body looks." She says.

"I've heard the cringe saying before, thanks," I say bluntly as I push her from me.

"What's got into you?" She snaps.

"Nothing," I say.

I grab my t-shirt from the bed and put it on. I walk out of my bedroom and leave Piper alone. I go into the bathroom and lock the door. I want more... I want to kill as much as I can and get away with it.

"I wonder if Piper was right? What if I have a major rage frenzy that it would stay permanent?" I ask myself.

"The rage frenzy is the only thing that makes me feel great, makes me feel something..." I mumble to myself.

I face the mirror and close my eyes. I begin to force myself to think of the worst possible things that can bring a major rage frenzy. Killian killing our parents, Killian torturing me, Quin telling me I'm like Killian. I think of them one by one. It starts immediately with the first memory. I begin to burn up, the burning headache appears, ringing in my ears. I open my eyes and look in the mirror and my pupils shrink, my nose begins to bleed. The rush that felt like a high appeared and stayed. I smile and begin to giggle.

"I feel amazing!" I yell.

I realize I don't sound the same. I sound like a crazy person, but that doesn't matter. My eyes began to bleed, I hate it.

"Why is this happening?" I growl into the mirror.

I grab some toilet paper and wipe the blood away. I wash my face with water. Then dry it with a towel. I quickly look back in the mirror, it has stopped.

"Yes! I still feel it and nothing is spoiling it!" I continue.

I open the bathroom door and run downstairs, I grab my hoodie from the coat rack and run out of the house.

Chapter 21

I Can't Snap Out of It!

I've not been home for 2 days, I've killed 3 people who I don't know. I sit underneath a tree in Dead Man's Woods, I cover my face with my hands, close my eyes, and rock back and forth.

"Let me... snap... out of... it!" I growl.

I hit my head and clench my teeth. But nothing is working. I grab my phone from my pocket and see I have hundreds of missed calls and voice messages. I don't care. I throw my phone at the tree in front of me and continues to try and get out of this permanent frenzy.

"Why can't I snap out of it!" I growl.

I stand up and begin to scream. It's my last and only option to try and release the built-up anger. I stop and fall to the floor on my hands and knees. I begin to take deep breaths in an attempt to calm myself. None of it worked. I still want to kill, I still want revenge. There is no way of going back. I stand up again and grab my phone from the side of the tree. It still worked. I put it in my pocket and head to Callie's.

I stand at the door and knock. I step back and wait for someone to answer. I throw my hood up and put my hands in my pockets. The door opens.

"Lockie! Where have you been?" Callie yells.

"Can... can I come in?" I stutter.

"Yeah, sure!" She says as she opens the door fully.

I walk in and look around. Exactly how I remember it the night she almost died because of that stupid curse.

"Are you alone?" I ask.

Callie nods and shows me into the living room. I walk in and sit down.

"Should I call your parents? They're worried about you." She asks as she stares at me.

"Don't!" I snap.

"What's got into you? You don't sound the same anymore..." She says worryingly.

I stand up from the couch and walk over to Callie. I place my hands on her cheeks and kiss her on the lips. I stop and pull away.

"New and improved me. Want to go upstairs?" I ask with a smile.

Callie nods and grabs my hand. She leads me to her bedroom, I close the door behind us.

"I'm going to have a bath; you can come with me if you want?" She asks with a smile.

"Sure..." I reply.

I follow her to her bathroom. Her bath is already ready. She starts to get undressed I sit on the toilet seat and watch. I smile and she smiles back at me. She climbs into the bath and lays down. I stand up and walk over then kneel beside the bath.

"You should join me." She giggles.

"No, I'm happy watching." I smile.

I watch her as she closes her eyes and relaxes. Quickly I lean over and pin her down under the water. She begins to kick and attempt to pull me off her, it didn't work. I hold her under until her body became limp. I grab a razor blade from my pocket I lift her left arm and cut vertically down her wrist the blood begins to pour into the water. I grab her other wrist and do the same. I pull the cloth from the tap and put it into the water, I wipe my prints from the blade and drop it in the water. I stand up and make my way out of her house. I open her bedroom door with the sleeve of my hoodie I head downstairs and do the same with the front door and closed it behind me. I make my way back to Dead Man's Woods.

My phone begins to vibrate. I pull it out of my pocket and look at the broken screen, it's Piper. I answer.

"Yeah?" I say.

"Where the hell are you?" She yells.

"I can't reveal that information," I say.

"Stop playing games, Lockie! Tell me where you are!" She continues.

"So you can tell mum and dad? No." I reply.

I hear her breathing heavily on the phone, it sounds like she is out looking for me.

"Just tell me for fuck sake!" She yells.

"Dead Man's Woods. You don't want to come near me." I warn.

"Ok, I'm on my way! And you're all I have that makes me feel like me, I need you." She says.

I pull the phone away from my ear and see my mum is trying to call me.

"Why won't they leave me alone?" I say.

"Because they care Lockie. They love you, I love you." She says softly.

"Don't come to me," I say as I stand up and begin to walk.

"Why? Stay there!" She yells.

"Piper, I have killed people who have come across me. I've finally snapped into a psychopath, stay away." I say.

I take the long route out of Dead Man's Woods. Walking in this direction I won't bump into Piper. I hang up and continue to ignore all the calls.

I can't control myself. I want to find Kil, I want him to die. I want to kill people who deserve to be killed. I need to plan something and fast. I walk towards the second exit of Dead Man's Woods and an idea came into my head.

"I need to get into the police system!" I thought.

I rush home, I haven't been back since I've become worse. Since I have killed my friends...

I get home and run upstairs into my bedroom. I get undressed and grab some fresh clothes. How am I going to explain being missing again?

Knock, knock

"Don't come in!" I yell.

"Where have you been?" My mum screams.

"I'll tell you in a minute! Give me a minute!" I yell back.

I quickly throw my dirty clothes under my mattress and silently put it down. I tiptoe to the door and open it.

"Yes?" I reply as I step towards her and close my door behind me.

"Where the hell have you been? Why are you acting as nothing has happened?" She continues.

"Shhh... I'm fine, I'm here, I'm unharmed... smile!" I say with a smile.

My mum pauses and stares at me. Her jaw drops open; her eyes widen in shock. I can't help but continue to give her a cheesy grin.

"Your dad will be home soon... we will discuss it further then..." She stutters.

I nod and watch her as she slowly drags her feet downstairs, still looking shocked as she takes a step at a time. She disappears out of sight and I breathe a sigh of relief and head into my room again. I close the door and run over to my desk. I open my laptop up and begin to search for recent murders, rapes, any criminal activity.

I've been on the search engine a while now and wrote down all the names of the criminals that have not yet been caught. I fold up the paper and place it into my phone case. I need names to faces for this to work.

I creep out of my bedroom and look around then proceed to the stairs. I jump the last step and happily stroll into the living room. There sits my mum and dad, as I walk into the room I see Quin standing by the kitchen door.

"I didn't know the freak show was in town?" I grumble.

"Where have you been?" My dad asks.

"Held captive by a psychopath as per usual." I lie.

Quin looks towards my mum and dad, then back at me.

"You do know your friends have died?" Quin asks.

"Well no, I've not been around for a week." I snap.

"Trey, Deccan, Callie... what's going on Lockie?" My mum asks.

I walk over to the couch and throw myself on it. I sit up and look at my parents.

"I don't know," I say bluntly as I fold my arms and cross my foot one over the other.

"There must be something? 2 are suicides and 1 is accidental..." My dad questions.

I shrug. I look over to Quin, I feel he knows something.

"I don't know what you're planning to get out of me but I know nothing... at all..." I continue.

"If you've been kidnapped again, you're holding it together well Lockie." Quin hints as he looks to my parents and folds his arms.

The stupid freak. He always has an answer for everything! He does make my blood boil.

"Do you want some more surgery added to your insurance for your face?" I ask with a smile.

"Lockie!" My dad yells.

"He's a nosey freak! He's always around when shit happens, why?" I yell.

"He can pick up on emotion and other things such as your aura." My dad continues.

"For the love of God!" I scream as I throw myself forward to stand up.

"Can you hear yourselves? You sound as crazy as a freak show over there!" I continue as I point to Quin.

"Something isn't right with you Lockie and we want to get to the bottom of it!" My dad yells.

I shake my head and head to the door and open it, I slam it shut behind me.

"I would rather be kidnapped than sit there listening to your bullshit!" I yell through the door as I open the front door. I jog down the driveway and follow the street. I hate being ridiculed.

I sit at a bus stop and grab the paper from the back of my phone case. I stare at it.

"Crime scene at a time," I mutter.

I unfold the paper and look at the first name, I smile then place it back into my phone case. I look up across the road, I'm not too far away from the crime scene address.

Nothing. How can I serve justice killing these disgusting people when I can't find them! I need a release; I need to kill someone. Then an idea appears in my head, Quin. I smile and follow the road back. Maybe he can be my final one until I can successfully kill prisoners to be.

I arrive on Quin's street, it's quiet. I sneak over to the front door as well as checking around me, no one is around. I pull my hoodie sleeve over my hand and I turn the handle and open the door, quietly I close it behind me and head into the side room. Suddenly I hear Quin in the living room next door to where I am. I smile, this is perfect. I turn and look around the room, I notice a shotgun on the wall. I tiptoe over and slowly lift it from the wall while still keeping my hands covered with my sleeves. I open it up and see it's loaded, I close it and walk round to the living room. I kick the door open and Quin stands up holding his hands up.

"Lockie!" He yells.

"Your time is up, Quin. I've had enough of your bullshit and twisting my parent's minds." I growl as I lift the shotgun aiming it at Quin's face.

"Lockie! This is not you, please stop!" He begs.

"The dead can't hear you." I smile.

I pull the trigger and instantly Quin's head blows up. His skull, brain, and blood splatter onto the wall behind, his body slumps to the floor with a thud.

"Hmm, you're not dead yet," I say as I point the shotgun to his abdomen.

One last shot and I blow a large hole into his stomach. Blood, mushy organs, and intestines spill out onto the floor.

"Say hi to the devil for me, you're in hell now." I smile as I turn to leave the room.

I walk out into the hallway holding the shotgun tightly in my sleeve. I look to the kitchen and follow it to the back door. I place my other sleeve over my hand and pull the handle down and leave through the yard. I drop the shotgun onto the floor with no prints, I climb over the fence and continue my escape walking the field behind Quin's home. I smile again and place my hands into my jean pockets.

"Ding, dong the prick is dead." I laugh.

TO BE CONTINUED...

Printed in Great Britain
by Amazon

60599143R00149